The Secret Tree

Natalie Standiford

SCHOLASTIC PRESS * NEW YORK

Library of Congress Cataloging-in-Publication Data available

ISBN 978-0-545-33479-2

10 9 8 7 6 5 4 3 2 1   12 13 14 15 16

Printed in the U.S.A.   23

First edition, May 2012

The text was set in Sabon MT.

Book design by Christopher Stengel

For: Sam, Willard,
and Big Natalie

THE LEGEND OF
THE SECRET TREE

A ghost can live anywhere. Some ghosts live in the water. Some haunt houses or graveyards. Others live in the air. And some ghosts live in the trees.

If a tree has a good, deep hole in its trunk, a ghost can live inside it, feeding on secrets. Secret-keepers are drawn to the tree. They put their secrets in the hole, the ghost eats them, and soon those people are free. Their secrets whisper from the branches of the tree and float away on the wind, gone forever.

Every town has its stories and superstitions. In Catonsville, we have Crazy Ike, the Witch House, the Man-Bat, and the Secret Tree. I stumbled upon the Secret Tree in the woods across from my house last summer. This is what happened.

CHAPTER 1
A Creature in the Woods

I'm Minty Fresh. My best friend is Pax A. Punch.

Minty Fresh and Pax A. Punch are not famous yet. But when we're older and rule roller derby, our names will bring fear to skaters all over the world.

Not that Minty Fresh is a very scary name.

Paz and I have been derby fans since we were eight, when our local roller rink started its own team, the Catonsville Nine. We cheered for them all winter — tough young women in helmets and knee pads, skating hard in competition against the Arbutus Cuties and the powerhouse Baltimore Bombers. We got our own roller skates and practiced tricks and skills.

I struggled to come up with my roller derby name. Minty Fresh didn't pack a punch like Pax A. Punch. It sounds like a toothpaste. But I hadn't been able to think of anything better.

"What about Cleo*pain*tra?" Paz suggested. We were skating in front of her house, in the loop that dead-ends our street. "Or Carrie A. Chainsaw?"

I tried them out. "Minty Mortimer, also known as *Cleopaintra*. No. Sorry. It just isn't me. It has nothing to do with my real name."

"So?"

She didn't get it. I wanted to turn myself into a roller derby superstar. My real self, not a made-up person.

She's lucky: Paz Anita Calderon is great material for a roller derby name. *Paz* means "peace" in Spanish, and *pax* means "peace" in Latin. They're basically the same word. And *A* is Paz's real middle initial! It's like her parents were thinking of roller derby when they named her. Though, knowing her parents, they probably weren't.

Lennie, Paz's younger sister, sat on the curb, keeping an eye on their little brothers, Hugo and Robbie, as they tumbled across the Calderons' front yard like puppies. "I've got one for you," Lennie said. "I. Minty Structable!" Lennie could sit around thinking up roller derby names all day.

"Too awkward," I said.

"Sheila Beecherbutt?" Lennie tried.

"It's getting dark," Paz said. "Let's do one more leg whip."

The leg whip is a trick we saw Lemon E. Kickit and Willa Steele do at the last Catonsville Nine bout. Willa stuck out one leg behind her, Lemon grabbed her foot, and Willa kicked it forward, whipping Lemon up the track to score a point. Lemon E. Kickit is a jammer, which means she scores points for her team by passing the other

team's skaters. The other skaters on the track are blockers, who try to keep the opposing jammer from scoring.
The trick is for the jammer to get past the enemy team's
blockers, and the leg whip worked great.

Paz skated ahead of me and stuck out her leg. I grabbed
her foot. She kicked me forward. Her long, black braid
whipped around her head, but I didn't whip anywhere. I
fell on my butt. Again.

"Great trick," Lennie said. "What's it called, the butt
bouncer? You should totally do it in the parade."

"The parade's two weeks away," I said. "We'll have it
down by then." I wasn't so sure. But I figured if I kept saying it, it might come true.

Paz and I planned to skate in the neighborhood's
annual Fourth of July Parade. We used to decorate our
bikes and ride around the block like all the other kids, but
this year we were going to blow everyone's minds with
our roller derby routine. If we could ever get it right.

"Let's go to the rink tomorrow for some real practice,"
I said, changing out of my skates.

"Can I skate with you?" Lennie pleaded. "I'm a mil-
lion times better than either one of you."

I knew what Paz would say. Lennie was right — she
was at least as good a skater as me or Paz. But she was
only nine. Ever since Paz turned eleven, she tried to leave
Lennie out of everything. Paz said Lennie was too young,
which made steam shoot out Lennie's ears.

"Maybe next year," Paz said. "I'm thirsty. Go get us some lemonade."

"Why should I?" Lennie's jaw jutted out.

"Because I asked you to," Paz said.

"You didn't ask me, you ordered me," Lennie said.

"If you don't want Mami and Papi to find out about *you know what*," Paz said, "then you'll get us some lemonade."

"Grrr." Lennie rose to her feet and went inside the house.

"What's *you know what*?" I asked Paz.

"She put a drink on the side table in the living room," Paz said. "And it left a ring."

"Oh." The Calderon kids weren't even supposed to *be* in the living room, much less leave rings on the mahogany furniture that had come all the way from the Philippines.

An ominous sound — *pfft pfft pfft*, like the blades of a distant chopper — came around the corner. It could only mean one thing.

The Mean Boys.

The Mean Boys, David Serrano and Troy Rogers, turned the corner on their dirt bikes. They *called* them dirt bikes, but they were just regular bicycles with fat tires and playing cards stuck in the spokes to make that *pfft pfft pfft* sound. They flashed their neon Super Soakers like gangsters.

"Oh Pa-a-a-z." Troy made kissing noises at her — *smack smack smack.*

"Hide!" Paz ran for Hugo and Robbie. But there wasn't time to hide.

"Hold it right there!" David shouted. He aimed his squirt gun at me and pulled the trigger. A red spray shot out of the gun.

"Hey!" My white T-shirt was splattered with sticky red juice.

"How about a nice Hawaiian Punch?" David laughed like a maniac. He sprayed Robbie and Hugo red. Troy zeroed in on Paz, yelling, "You can run, but you can't hide!"

Quick as they'd come, the Mean Boys disappeared down Western Street to Carroll Drive, where they both lived. Paz, Robbie, Hugo, and I were left dripping and sticky.

Lennie came out of the house, balancing four paper cups full of lemonade in her hands. "The Mean Boys?" She handed a cup to Paz. "Your Majesty."

"Thank you." Paz took her cup and sipped.

"You're lucky you missed it, Lennie," I said.

"Lennie always has such interesting timing," Paz said. "I bet she knew the Mean Boys were coming."

I took a lemonade from Lennie and settled on the curb to wait out another sister smackdown. Paz and Lennie had been fighting for as long as I'd known them, and that was a long time. The Calderons moved to Catonsville from the Philippines before I started first grade. Paz was in my class, and we became instant best friends.

Now we were going into sixth grade. We were about to start middle school together.

Lennie glared at Paz. "It wasn't my idea to go inside. You ordered me to get you lemonade. I bet you wanted to be alone with your boyfriend, Troy."

"Don't make me puke," Paz said. "You're the one who likes Troy."

"You guys, nobody likes Troy." I was hoping this would stop the argument, but it didn't work.

I stared into the woods across the street, trying to ignore them. It was that after-dinner hour when the world looks like a black-and-white movie. The grass turned gray, the lemonade white, and the red stain on my T-shirt blackened as the light drained away.

The woods rustled. Some kind of creature moved among the low trees that bordered our street. I could see the leaves shaking, but I couldn't tell what was hiding in there.

"What are you staring at?" Paz asked me.

"I thought I saw something," I said.

A branch snapped. I could make out an arm and a small blob that might have been a head. The rest of the creature blended in with the leaves.

Flash! A light sparked in the woods.

"Hey!" Paz said. "Did someone just take our picture?"

Lennie clutched my arm. "The Man-Bat!"

"Calm down," Paz said.

"Does the Man-Bat make flashes like that?" I asked Lennie.

"His eyes are yellow-green. He could flash them if he wanted to."

Lennie was obsessed with the Man-Bat, a giant half man, half bat who supposedly lived in the woods. He was seven feet tall with webbed hands and feet and could fly like a bat. He attacked people and animals. Sometimes he rattled people's windows, trying to get inside their houses.

Another *flash!* Paz shaded her eyes. "What *is* that?"

I jumped up. "I'm going to find out."

"Minty, don't!" Lennie tugged on my arm. "The Man-Bat skins squirrels alive!"

"I'm not a squirrel," I said. "And I want to know what's making that flash."

I took a deep breath and barreled into the woods.

CHAPTER 2
A Whispering Tree

The creature crashed away through the trees. He was fast and hard to see, but I could tell he wasn't seven feet tall like the Man-Bat. He was closer to my size.

"Stop!" I yelled. "Get back here!" The creature ran like he was being chased by an ax murderer. Soon he disappeared in the deep dark of the woods. I got about halfway through before I had to stop and catch my breath.

It was full-on night now. A few lightning bugs flickered through the trees. Otherwise, darkness. I listened for the creature. He was gone.

There was another noise, though . . . a murmur that burbled under the creaks of cicadas and crickets and birds, the breeze shuffling the leaves, the yelps of kids, and the roar of traffic far away . . . a murmur like voices, whispering.

I took a step toward the sound, then another.

It was close by.

It swelled.

I was almost there.

I found myself in front of a big, old elm tree. It had a hole in its trunk bigger than my head, and when I pressed my hand against its thick bark, it vibrated like a hive full of bees.

I peered into the hole. It was dark inside the tree, but a bit of white winked in the blackness.

There were no bees. Just that scrap of white. I reached into the hole and pulled out a piece of paper, folded up many times.

What was a piece of paper doing inside a tree?

"Minty!" Paz shouted. Her voice seemed to come from far away. "Where are you? Come back!"

I stuffed the paper in my shorts pocket and ran back through the woods. When they saw me, Hugo and Robbie jumped up and down and waved. "Yay! The Man-Bat didn't get her!"

"Are you okay?" Paz asked.

"He got away," I said.

"Who got away?" Lennie asked.

"I'm not sure, but I think it was a boy," I told them. "Sorry, Lennie, but he wasn't tall enough to be the Man-Bat."

"Don't say sorry." Lennie shook her head. "I don't *want* it to be the Man-Bat. But it could have been a Boy-Bat."

"Maybe," I said, to make her feel better.

"That flash," Paz said. "Why would he want to take our picture?"

"He must be a spy," Hugo said. "He was spying on us!"

"Where did he go?" Lennie asked.

"He ran to the other side of the woods," I reported. "All the way through." I didn't mention the tree that stopped me along the way. It was like the tree had told me in its murmur to keep it a secret.

"The other side . . ." The Calderons all turned their eyes nervously to the woods.

There was only one place a person could go on the other side of the woods.

The Witch House.

"He couldn't live there," Hugo said. "No one lives there but the Witch Lady. And she eats children."

If the Man-Bat was a legend — I couldn't be sure, but I'd never seen any proof that he wasn't — the Witch House was one hundred percent real.

"I don't like being spied on," Paz said. She clutched her stomach. "Ow."

"What's wrong?" I asked.

"My stomach hurts." Paz sank onto the grass and rolled over on her side. "Oof."

"Did you do something to it?" I asked.

"No. Everything was fine. Then right after the Mean Boys were gone — pow. Ug. Ow . . ."

"Oh, no!" Lennie said. "Are you okay?"

"I'll get Awa." Hugo ran inside. Awa is the Calderons' cook. She doesn't speak much English, but she knows strange herbal cures for everything from bee stings to poison ivy to headaches.

I knelt beside Paz, who moaned and rolled back and forth, her face squished with pain. "I don't understand it," I said. "How did you get so sick all of a sudden?"

"I don't know. . . ."

Awa ran outside, trailed by Hugo. Muttering in Chinese, she examined Paz, staring into her eyes and poking at her stomach. She said something else in Chinese — the Calderon kids can usually understand her, even though they don't speak much Chinese themselves. She helped Paz to her feet and led her into the house. I started to follow them, but then the bell rang — my parents calling me home with an old ship's bell they'd hung in our backyard.

"I'll get my dad," I said. "I'll be right back."

My dad is an emergency room doctor, and my mom teaches nursing at the community college, so they're like the neighborhood medics.

"That's okay," Lennie said. "Awa has it under control."

"Awa," I called. Awa turned. "Should I get my dad?" I pointed down the street toward my house, three doors away, where the bell was insistently ringing.

Awa shook her head. "No, no, is okay."

I frowned. Awa knew what she was doing, but I was worried about Paz. "Lennie, call my dad if you need him. Promise?"

"I promise," Lennie said. Awa nodded and waved me away. They all disappeared inside the Calderon house, leaving me alone in the front yard, the ship's bell ringing and ringing. I walked home, thinking about Paz and the Witch House.

CHAPTER 3
Halloween at the Witch House

We live on Woodlawn Road, a dead-end street, one side lined with cookie-cutter houses, the other side lined with woods. Behind our houses are more houses and more streets, like Carroll Drive, where the Mean Boys live.

On the other side of the woods, for as long as anyone could remember, an old farmhouse sat rotting and lonely, surrounded by barren fields. It was tall and shabby, with peeling paint, cobwebs in the dusty windows, and gray shingles missing from the roof. Everyone called it the Witch House.

A crazy lady lived in the house. As far as we knew, she was as scary, rotten, and alone as her house. Last Halloween, Troy Rogers dared me, Paz, and Lennie to ring the Witch Lady's doorbell and say, "Trick or treat!" We didn't want to do it, but Troy said if we didn't, he'd egg us until we were walking omelets.

So we agreed to do it. "We'll just press the doorbell, say 'trick or treat,' and run like crazy," Lennie said. "We won't even wait for the door to open."

"I guess it can't hurt anyone," I said.

For Halloween I'd dressed up as my favorite roller derby superstar, Lemon E. Kickit, in black-and-gold Catonsville Nine's colors, with a gold helmet and a black mask to hide my eyes. Lennie decided to go as a bat, in case we ran into the Man-Bat that night. She figured he wouldn't hurt her if he thought they might be related.

Paz had planned to go as her derby favorite, Willa Steele, but changed her mind at the last minute and had dressed up as, of all things, a witch — a *cute* witch — in a silky, black dress. She already has long, black hair, so no wig was necessary. She taped Lennie's toy cat, Marcella, to her shoulder. "Every witch needs a familiar," she explained.

Lennie had had Marcella since she was a baby. She protested strenuously.

"You can't take Marcella," she said to Paz. "What if something happens to her?"

"Nothing will happen to her."

"I can't fall asleep without her," Lennie whispered. I don't think she wanted me to hear that.

"I said, nothing will happen."

"It better not, or you'll be sorry," Lennie said.

"Ooh, I'm so scared."

That Halloween night we marched through the neighborhood, stopping at every house from Woodlawn Road to Western Street to Carroll Drive to Bailey Street. When our bags were stuffed with candy, we dropped them off at the Calderons' house and started our trek through the woods. I changed out of my roller skates, since it's hard to run through the woods on wheels and I wanted to be able to make a quick escape.

The night was chilly and clear. An owl hooted high above us. "I heard that owl tried to swoop down and snatch up Kelly," Lennie said. Kelly is our neighbor Mrs. Gorelick's dog, a wheezy little Pekingese. "Luckily, Mr. Gorelick scared it away. But it sits in the woods across from their yard, watching and waiting for Kelly to come out."

"Quiet, Lennie," Paz said. "You're giving me the creeps."

Lennie's small laugh had a touch of evil in it.

We crunched over the carpet of leaves, weaving through the trees until we got to the edge of the woods. The Witch House rose tall and dark from fields frosted with moonlight.

"All right," Paz said grimly. "Let's go."

Marcella wobbled on her shoulder as we skittered toward the dark porch. A single light glowed in a back window — the kitchen, I guessed — and smoke puffed out of the chimney.

Someone was home.

We took the three front steps slowly, but they *creak, creak, creaked*. The porch light wasn't on.

"I guess she's not expecting trick-or-treaters," I whispered.

"Shh!" Paz said. "Just ring the bell and get it over with."

"*You* ring it," Lennie said.

"I'll do it." I reached for the doorbell. Just as my finger touched it . . . *whap*! An egg smacked against the front door and dripped yellowly down the wood.

"The Mean Boys!" Lennie shouted.

I ducked as another egg burst against the window just over my head, cracking the glass.

"Ha-ha! Gotcha!" David whooped.

Paz ducked behind the porch railing as an egg whizzed past her. Lennie and I ran into the yard to chase the Mean Boys away.

The porch light suddenly flashed on. The Mean Boys threw one more egg at the house and vanished into the woods. Lennie and I hid behind a bush.

"Paz!" I shouted, but she cowered on the porch, frozen with fear, just outside the puddle of light.

The front door flew open and a wild-haired woman stepped out, shrieking, "I'm calling the police!" She wore a ratty bathrobe and a cat mask over her eyes. Maybe she was getting ready to go to a party. Maybe she was celebrating Halloween in her own way. Maybe she was crazy.

She spotted Paz huddled on the porch and lunged for her. "You!" she screeched. "You!" She grabbed at Paz, ripping Marcella from her shoulder. Paz screamed and finally found her legs, scrambling off the porch and racing for the woods. Lennie and I were way ahead of her.

"You!" The Witch Lady called again. "Curse you kids!"

We ran without stopping all the way through the woods. The Mean Boys were waiting on the other side, laughing at the fear on our faces.

"You were the first ones to run," I reminded them.

"We weren't running because we were scared," Troy said. "It was all part of the setup." They hopped on their bikes. "We've got more tricking to do. Later, girls."

They zipped away, the cards in their wheel spokes *pfft pfft pffting*.

"We should have known they were setting us up," Paz said.

"Hey." Lennie reached for Paz's shoulder. "Where's Marcella?"

Paz swallowed. Lennie hadn't seen what had happened.

"Paz? Did she fall off in the woods?"

"Lennie —" I began.

"Let's go look for her," Lennie said.

"The Witch Lady got her," Paz confessed. "She ripped her right off my shoulder."

Lennie's mouth dropped open in horror. She isn't the crying type, but I could tell she was fighting off tears. "Marcella . . ."

"We'll get her back, Lennie," I said.

"How? The Witch Lady's keeping her prisoner! Who's got the nerve to go back there and get her?"

"It's not worth risking *that* again," Paz said. "It's just

a toy, Len. You're getting too old to sleep with stuffed animals, anyway."

Lennie glared at Paz through wet eyes, a defiant, angry look that scared me. "You don't care. You don't care about me at all. You're a terrible sister."

"Lennie —"

Lennie ran home. Paz turned to me. "Well? Are you going to yell at me too?"

"You didn't mean to lose Marcella," I said.

"Exactly. Thank you." Paz looked down at the sidewalk, her lower lip twitching. If she felt sad or guilty, she'd never admit it.

"What did she look like?" I asked. "The Witch Lady. Up close, I mean."

"Her hair was all tangly, and she smelled like beer," Paz said. "And she was missing a tooth right *here*." Paz pointed to her upper right canine tooth. "She had a big hole there. But it was hard to see much of her face because she had that mask on."

"She got a good look at you, though."

Paz's lip twitched again. "You think so?"

"You're the only one she saw, I guess."

"Yeah." Paz tugged on a strand of hair and put it in her mouth, sucking on it. Her mother had been trying to get her to break that habit, and I hadn't seen her do it in ages. "But she can't do anything to me, right? We weren't the ones throwing eggs."

"She doesn't know that."

"Minty, are you trying to scare me? Quit it."

We walked back to her house. I picked up my candy and went home.

Lennie never got Marcella back. None of us had been to the other side of the woods since that night. It was too scary. I'd hardly even thought about the Witch Lady. . . .

Until now.

CHAPTER 4
The First Secret

I crossed Western Street and walked past the Murphys' house, where Kip and Casey live, past the home of Ms. Wendy Graecher, who lives with her cat, Phoebe, to Mortimer Mansion. That's what Dad calls our house, even though it isn't anything like a mansion. It's just a regular house like all the others on Woodlawn Road.

Dad was sitting at the picnic table on the back patio, a glass of iced tea sweating on the wood, watching the lightning bugs wink in the yard.

"What's the news, Araminta?" He eyed my red-stained clothes. "I hope that's not blood."

I knew Dad was joking, because if anyone knows what blood looks like, it's him. As a doctor, he sees gallons of it every day. I could never be a doctor, because if the red stuff on my shirt had been blood, I'd have been puking by now.

"It's Hawaiian Punch," I told him.

I heard shouting through the screen door. Mom and Thea, my big sister, were fighting again. No wonder Dad had decided to sit outside.

"What now?" I asked.

"Curfew," Dad said. "Thea wants to stay out until midnight tonight."

Thea was fifteen. She had a part-time summer job teaching arts and crafts at a day camp. Her usual curfew was ten o'clock.

I sat down and sipped Dad's iced tea. He put his arm around me.

"I hope I won't turn out like Thea when I get older," I said.

"I doubt you will," Dad said. "You're a different creature, Minty."

Speaking of creatures . . . "We saw a weird flash in the woods," I told him. "I chased after it, but I couldn't tell what it was. Lennie thinks it was the Man-Bat."

Dad looked at me. "You shouldn't have chased it, Minty. You don't know who that might have been."

"Whoever it was, he ran away. And he wasn't very tall. I think it was a kid."

"Strange." Dad scratched the stubble on his face. He needed a shave.

"Then Paz got a stomachache," I said. "I told them to call you if they need to."

"I'm sure she'll be fine." That's what he always said. "I've got to go to the hospital later tonight. They can bring her in if the pain doesn't go away." Dad worked long, odd hours, and lots of nights.

I heard Thea stomp down the stairs. We both turned our heads as the front door slammed. Mom appeared at the back door, her face red from shouting.

"Where's she going?" Dad asked.

"To tell Melina all about her terrible mother," Mom said. Melina is Paz's older sister and Thea's best friend. Usually, Thea complains to her about *me*. "Minty Mortimer, time for your bath."

I stood up. Dad gave me a pat. I followed Mom upstairs. The bathwater was already running.

In my room, I took off my grubby T-shirt and shorts. I checked my shorts pocket before tossing them into the hamper and found the piece of paper from the tree in the woods. The running bathwater sounded almost like the murmur. I felt a slight breeze run through the room, or maybe it was just inside of me. I got goose bumps.

I unfolded the paper and read what had been written there.

No one loves me except my goldfish.

CHAPTER 5
The Story of Crazy Ike

I soaked in the tub as the bathwater cooled, wondering who could have written that note. Maybe the mysterious flashing creature left it there. After all, he'd been lurking in that part of the woods when I'd caught him spying on us.

I said it out loud: "No one loves me except my goldfish." Back in my bedroom, my own goldfish, Zuzu, restlessly circled the bowl on my dresser. Every kid in the neighborhood had a goldfish. Mr. Jack, who lived next door to Troy, owned a pet store, and he gave everyone a goldfish on his or her birthday.

Anyone could have written that note. But who could be so terribly lonely?

The Calderons were such a big family, I didn't see how any one of them could feel unloved. Thea had Melina, and I had Paz. Even Hugo and Robbie had each other, and Lennie had me and Paz.

I couldn't imagine either of the Mean Boys writing a note like that. Could a grown-up have written it? Wendy Graecher lived alone next door, and she was always going on bad dates with men she met online. She had a gold-fish, but she also had her cat, Phoebe, and I knew Phoebe loved her.

Maybe the note was a secret code, or a message. The hole in the tree could be a spy drop-off point, which meant the mystery creature really was a spy, and he left coded secret messages in the tree for his contact to pick up in the middle of the night. Who could he be working for? The government? A spy agency? Aliens?

But why spy on *us*? All we did was roller-skate and play kickball. I couldn't see how some foreign government would be interested in that. Or aliens.

And then I remembered Mr. and Mrs. Calderon. They worked in Washington, DC, at the Philippine embassy.

Someone might want some secrets about the Philippines. Or maybe they were planning to kidnap the Calderon children! And demand the secrets in exchange for their release!

I couldn't soak another minute. I got out of the tub and put on my summer pajamas. Back in my room, I stashed the secret note in my special treasure box, along with a lock of my hair from my first haircut, a ticket stub from my first Orioles game, a program from the first Catonsville Nine bout I ever went to, Lemon E. Kickit's autograph, my collection of Paz's school pictures from first through fifth grades, and a turquoise ring Paz gave me that had broken. The note wasn't a treasure, exactly, but it seemed important, something I should keep safe and hidden. I might need it someday.

I got into bed and tried to read. But my mind wouldn't settle down — thoughts about secrets and spies kept swirling through my brain. Someone knocked on the door. "Come in."

It was Dad. "I wanted to say good night before I leave for work." He sat on my bed. He smelled good. He'd just shaved.

"Dad, do you think that person in the woods was spying on us?" I asked.

"Spies? Around here? I don't know about that. Maybe it was Crazy Ike." Dad made a spooky face. I shrank deeper under the covers with a happy shiver. He loved to tell the story of Crazy Ike. He used to hear about Crazy Ike when he was growing up, not far from where we lived now.

"Who's Crazy Ike?" I asked, as if I didn't know the story by heart.

"Who's Crazy Ike?" Dad repeated. "Funny you should ask. Ike was a boy who lived a long time ago on a farm on the other side of the woods — just over there." Dad jerked his thumb toward the woods across the street. "He lived in the very same house they call the Witch House today."

"Is that a fact?" I asked.

"That's a bona fide historical fact," Dad said. "It was a farmhouse back in those days. They had chickens and grew corn in the fields around the house. Ike was always kind of crazy. He tried to ride the plow horse standing up, which never worked well. And he smoked a corncob pipe from the age of five, they say."

"That's awfully young to start smoking," I said, playing along.

"Any age is too young to start smoking," Dad said. "Take it from your doctor. Anyway, Ike made up lots of stories about himself. Some might call them lies."

"Like what?"

"Like once he said a bear ran into the kitchen and ate all the mincemeat pie — when his own face was covered in molasses and pie crumbs. And once he told his father he couldn't do chores because a monster was hiding in the chicken coop."

"Was there really a monster in the chicken coop?" I asked.

"What do you think?" Dad laughed. "That's not all. When a cinder from his pipe set fire to a haystack, he blamed a fire-breathing dragon. And when his teacher punished him for talking back in school, he said he didn't do it — a ghost had possessed his body and forced him to sass her. His mother and father never knew when to believe him."

"Uh-oh." I knew what was coming.

"One day, Ike claimed he'd been bitten by a bat. His parents thought he was telling one of his stories. But Ike got crazier and crazier. He flew into a rage over nothing. He threw pitchforks at people from the hayloft. He started foaming at the mouth. Finally, his father got the doctor. And the doctor said —"

"— Ike had rabies."

"That's right. There was no cure for rabies in those days. There's no cure now, but you'll be all right if you get vaccinated in time."

"Did they have the vaccine back then?" I asked.

"They had it, but it wasn't always easy to get," Dad said. "Not for poor farm boys, anyway."

"So what happened to Ike?"

"He went crazy and died at the tender age of twelve. They say he's buried on that land to this day, with nothing but a rock to mark his grave."

"Poor Ike."

"Yes indeed. Poor Crazy Ike. Some say he rose from his grave and grew into a Man-Bat: part man, part bat. A monster who lives in a cave in the woods —"

"Paul, don't scare her like that." Mom was standing in the doorway, listening.

"Lennie talks about the Man-Bat all the time," I said. "I'm used to it."

"I don't want you having nightmares about Man-Bats or Crazy Ike," Mom said.

"Or international spies," I added.

"Or anything at all," she finished.

Dad kissed me. "Good night, Minty. See you tomorrow."

Mom kissed me too. "Good night, honey. Don't stay up too late reading."

"I won't," I lied. It was summer. I considered it my duty to stay up as late as my sleepy eyes would let me.

When I finally fell asleep, I didn't dream of the Man-Bat, or Crazy Ike, or international spies.

I dreamed about a goldfish swimming in a bowl all alone.

Chapter 6

A Theft at the Roller Rink

The next day, my life was one sentence different than it had been the day before. I kept looking at people I was used to seeing every day, and I wondered whether they felt that nobody loved them except their goldfish. Or if they were international spies.

It was rainy, so Thea and Melina took us all — me, Paz, Lennie, Hugo, and Robbie — to the Oella Roller Rink. Paz looked a little pale, but her stomach was all better.

"Did you ever figure out why it hurt so bad?" I asked.

Paz just shook her head.

We changed out of our sneakers and into our roller skates. We always brought our own skates instead of renting. We came to the rink so often that we had discount memberships, complete with photo ID. We stashed our membership cards in our sneakers and left them under a bench.

Thea and Melina helped Robbie and Hugo put on their skates. "The Carters asked me to babysit again," Thea told Melina. "It's good money. Plus the kids are cute. Not like that nightmare Troy Rogers." She shuddered. "I'll never sit for him again. Not after what happened last time."

Last time Troy had trained his cat, Slayer, to hide on a shelf in the pantry and leap out whenever the door opened. Every time Thea went to get something to eat — Troy was constantly asking for more nacho chips — Slayer would jump on her head. She had claw marks all over her shoulders when she got home.

"I need some money," Melina said. "I don't mind babysitting if I get paid, but I'd rather be a lifeguard. My whole life is babysitting. For free." She nodded at her younger brothers and sisters, lined up like ducks on the bench.

"Hey," Paz protested. "I watch them a lot too."

"I know the real reason you want to be a lifeguard," Lennie said to Melina. "Kip Murphy."

Kip Murphy was sixteen and lifeguarded at the Rollingwood Pool. Girls were always circling around his chair, distracting him from his lifesaving work.

Melina turned red. "That's not true. I'm very concerned with water safety, fitness, and saving lives."

"Pfff," Lennie scoffed.

"Robbie, stop kicking," Thea said.

"Anyway, I was talking about having to watch *you*," Melina said.

"You don't have to watch me anymore," Paz said. "I'm in middle school now."

"Not until September," Melina said. "And anyway, big deal."

"You're still a baby until you've *survived* middle school," Thea said. "At least a year of it."

"Yeah, wait till you see," Melina warned. "Bullies roam the halls bonking kids with their backpacks —"

"— and snapping girls' bra straps," Thea added. "If you're wearing one." She glanced at me.

"I'm comfortable with who I am." Somehow my arms ended up crossed over my chest. I didn't need a bra yet. I wasn't in any hurry to get one, either. Paz already had three training bras in DayGlo colors.

"Everything changes in middle school," Thea said. "Girls you thought were your friends suddenly turn mean on you —"

"Feuds break out everywhere," Melina said.

"— and then you have to find new friends."

"What about you guys?" Paz said. "You're still friends."

"We're the exception," Melina said. "Best friends forever." She reached across Hugo to fist-bump Thea.

"Get your fist out of my face," Hugo grumbled.

"Even if you keep your best friend," Thea said, "everything else changes."

"Your world gets rocked like an earthquake," Thea said.

Mr. Gorelick started playing "Shake Your Booty" on his Mighty Wurlitzer organ. I grabbed Paz by the hand and led her onto the rink. "Come on, Pax A. Punch — they're playing our song."

My next-door neighbor, Mr. Gorelick, was the house organist for the Oella Roller Rink. He played old disco tunes some afternoons and during the roller derby bouts. I grew up hearing all those old '70s songs blasting out of his house while he practiced. (His other hobby was polishing his 1929 Model A Ford Roadster, which he called Old Donna.)

"Hey there, girls!" Mr. Gorelick waved at us as we skated past the organ booth. "Keep those elbows sharp!"

After a warm-up run around the rink, Paz and I practiced another trick we were planning for the Fourth of July Parade: the Tunnel. So far we'd only done it right once. Paz skated in front of me and reached back between her legs to grab my hands. I crouched down and she pulled me through her legs until I stood up in front of her. Then I reached back and pulled her through my legs.

"Try not to polish the floor with your butt this time," Paz instructed.

"I'm not *trying* to polish the floor with my butt," I said.

She glided in front of me and reached between her legs for my hands. I grabbed them. I could always do that part. It was the next part that tripped me up.

I plopped to the floor. It was now a little more polished than it had been one second earlier.

"You guys are awesome," Lennie sneered as she speed-skated past us. "Minty Fresh and Pax A. Punch, go go go!"

"Get her," Paz muttered. We chased after Lennie, the meanest skaters on our imaginary roller derby team. I raced ahead and tagged Lennie on the back.

"Minty Fresh scores!" I raised my arms and turned around to get Paz's approval. But she wasn't there.

She had drifted over to the sidelines to talk to three girls: Isabelle Barton, Katie Park, and Lydia Kendall. They were going into seventh grade. They all wore the same silver barrettes, three of them lined up on one side of their hair, one barrette for each girl. Three girls, three barrettes each. Like a code for a secret club.

I rolled over to them. "Minty Fresh scored!"

For one second, Paz didn't look at me. She didn't say anything. It was like a strange, slow-motion delay. One second.

I shuddered.

Something was different. I felt it.

When the longest second in the history of time was finally over, Paz turned her head, blinked, and smiled at me. Same old Paz. Only not. Pax A. Punch was gone.

"We only came because it's raining, and there's nothing else to do," Isabelle was saying.

"This place is so cheesy," Lydia added. "I can't believe that old guy is still playing that stupid organ. Can't they get a DJ?"

"It smells like dirty socks in here." Katie sniffed.

These girls were too cool for goldfish. They had probably gotten rid of them a long time ago.

"Well, we're here. We might as well skate." Isabelle glided out onto the floor and demonstrated a beautiful figure-skating spin. It was not the kind of spin a roller derby girl would do. It was the kind of spin a roller derby girl would make fun of.

"Ooh," Katie and Lydia said.

"Ah," Paz sighed.

I held my tongue.

The Pax A. Punch I knew wouldn't ooh and ah over a girly spiral spin.

"It's not hard," Isabelle said. "I can show you."

Paz, Katie, and Lydia gathered around for a demonstration. I tried to squeeze in, but somehow there wasn't enough room in the circle for me.

"I'm getting a snowball," I said, frustrated. "Want one, Paz?"

Paz didn't answer. Isabelle was helping her bend backward for a spiral.

I skated over to the snack bar by myself and got a spearmint snowball. Spearmint is my favorite snowball flavor, not just because it matches my name. Then I sat in the bleachers to slurp it. Thea's bag was open, so I reached down to zip it up.

"Hey!" Thea dashed to the side of the rink. She's very aware of where her stuff is and who's touching it at all times. "Quit touching my stuff, Minty!"

"I'm not touching it," I said. "I was zipping it closed."

"Just don't touch it." She turned to Melina and said, "I hate when she does that. Does Paz have this obsession with touching your things?"

Melina nodded and laughed as they skated away together, commiserating over how horrible it is to have little sisters. That was a big part of their friendship — complaining about me and Paz.

Isabelle organized a game of Crack the Whip. She and her friends were tall girls, and Paz was almost as tall. I felt shrimpy next to them.

I finished my snowball fast — too fast, because I got brain freeze — and hurried back to the rink. Mr. Gorelick was playing "Get Down Tonight," and the disco ball was flashing colored lights.

I raced to catch up with the whip and grabbed Paz at the very end. We snaked around the oval, led by Isabelle. Suddenly the whip cracked, and I went flying into the bumper. Polishing the floor with my butt as usual. Everybody laughed, including me. I got up, brushed myself off, and scrambled to catch up to the whip as it whirled past me again.

David and Troy whizzed by, buzzing too close to Isabelle. "Hey!" Isabelle snapped. "You almost bumped me!"

The Mean Boys laughed and made rude noises. They stuck out their butts and made fun of the way we skated.

The whip waved across the rink, girls clinging to one another's slippery hands. I skated fast, trying to catch the tail, but before I could reach it, the Mean Boys zoomed by. Troy ducked under Isabelle's arm. She stumbled, wobbled, and let go of Lydia's hand behind her. Lydia bumped into Katie, who crashed into Lennie, who fell on top of Paz. In a chain reaction, the whip collapsed to the floor.

"Skate much?" David cackled.

Isabelle rubbed her knee. "I hate those Mean Boys," Paz muttered.

"Life would be so much nicer without them," Lennie added.

"Don't worry," Isabelle said. "Sixth grade will eat them alive."

Melina waved to us from the bleachers. "Time to go home," Lennie said.

I helped Paz to her feet, and we all skated back to the bench. "Bye, Paz," Isabelle said. "See you at the pool."

"Next sunny day," Paz promised.

We sat on the bench. Paz seemed to be avoiding my eyes. We sat quietly as we untied our skates.

Paz pulled her sneakers out from under the bench and reached inside one of them, then the other. Then the first again. Then the second again.

"Where's my ID?" she asked. She felt around inside her shoes one more time. Then she crouched down and looked under the bench. I looked too. I found my own ID inside my right sneaker, just where I'd left it.

"It's gone," Paz said. "Someone stole my ID!"

"Who'd want to do that?" I asked.

"Probably some maniac," Lennie said. "Like the Man-Bat."

Paz scowled. "I'm sure that's the most likely explanation."

"What's the difference between the Man-Bat and Batman?" Hugo asked.

"Who cares?" Paz said. "Help me find my ID!"

"Batman is a superhero. He helps people," Lennie said. "The Man-Bat is a monster. Like Bigfoot or Mothman or, I don't know, the Witch Lady. He hurts people."

Paz looked all over the rink. She checked the lost and found. But she couldn't find her ID. She reported it missing, and the manager gave her a temporary one.

"So what? You lost your ID," Lennie said as we walked home. "You'll get another one."

"That's not the point," Paz said. "The point is somebody took it. And the question is: Why?"

"You always make a big deal out of everything," Lennie told her. "Stop being such a drama queen."

"If someone stole something from you, you'd be screaming bloody murder," Paz pointed out.

Paz and Lennie bickered the rest of the way home. I hung back, thinking about the missing ID and wondering if this was connected to the other strange events of the last few days.

I didn't know it then, but it was.

CHAPTER 7
A Prowler

The next day was muggy and hot. I kicked open the screen door and sat on the front steps. The cicadas whined, which made the hot day seem to boil. I sucked on an orange Popsicle, trying to finish it before it melted. It dripped onto the brick step. In seconds, a line of ants crawled out of a crack in the brick and circled the sticky, orange drop.

It was already the end of June. When school let out, the whole summer had seemed to stretch out in front of me endlessly, and now the first month was practically gone.

It's funny how time goes so slowly at the beginning of summer. I noticed little summery things I'd forgotten about during the winter, like how the heat looks like oil rising off the black tar driveway, how mosquito bites itch the worst on your knuckles, and how ants march across the sidewalk in a straight line. How good orange Popsicles taste in the sun.

Orange Popsicles. Orange goldfish.

Funny how I could walk through the woods I'd known my whole life and suddenly find a tree I'd never noticed before — a tree with a strange note inside that made me start wondering about the people who lived around me, loved and unloved. I was jolted out of this thoughtful mood by a clank in the garage. I sat up, imagining robbers. Intruders. Man-Bats.

The garage door was wide open. There was another clank. Someone was in there.

"Thea?" I called. Maybe Thea was knocking around in the garage for some reason. It wasn't like her, but stranger things had happened. "Mom?"

No one answered. There were no more clanks. But I knew I'd heard something.

I crept up to the garage. What if it was a thief? What if someone was trying to steal my bike?

What if the Man-Bat was lying in wait?

I tiptoed up to the garage, whispering, "There's no such thing as a Man-Bat. There's no such thing as a Man-Bat. . . ." Curse that Lennie Calderon.

I paused. There was a cardboardy, papery sound, like someone rummaging. I tilted forward and peered into the dark garage.

A boy crouched on his knees on the floor, digging through a box of stuff Mom was going to throw out. He looked up at me with big raccoon eyes. His head was shaved nearly bald, and he wore green camouflage, like a soldier. A chunky, black plastic thing hung from a cord around his neck.

"Who are you?" I asked. "What are you doing?"

"Yáh!" he shouted. He jumped up, did a quick karate kick in the air, and streaked out of the garage before I had time to react. He ran straight into the woods.

"Stop! Stop!" I chased him. He was a very fast runner, and the camouflage made him blend into the trees. I thought I lost him for a second, but he reappeared in a patch of sunlight far ahead of me.

I was sure I'd never seen him before.

About three-quarters of the way into the woods, the boy stopped. He turned around, breathing hard. I ducked behind a tree to hide, hoping he'd think he wasn't being followed anymore. I wanted to see where he would go.

He caught his breath and looked around carefully. I didn't move. At last he decided it was safe and walked the rest of the way through the woods. I crept after him, trying my best not to make any noise.

He emerged from the trees into the bright, shadeless light of the other side. I stopped at the edge in shock.

The other side of the woods had been transformed. The Witch House was still there. But everything around it had changed.

The fields around the Witch House had been flattened and divided into plots, and on each plot stood a half-finished, brand-new house. The walls were wrapped in plastic covering printed with the word TYVEK, and the houses were missing roofs, doors, floors. The muddy yards were strewn with straw and a few shoots of young grass. One finished house sat at the entrance to the development with a sign that said MODEL HOME.

A whole new neighborhood was being built across the woods from us. But why did it look so forlorn and abandoned? Where were the construction workers?

I stayed hidden in the woods and watched the boy. He walked up to the Witch House and tried the front door. I wanted to shout, *Don't go in there!* But the boy didn't look scared. He rattled the doorknob again. It was locked. There was no sign of the Witch Lady.

The boy sat down on the front porch and pulled something small and flat — a piece of paper? — out of his pocket. He looked at it for a while.

Dong, dong, dong . . . The sound of the old ship's bell reached me all the way through the woods. Mom was ringing for me. She'd kill me if I didn't go home right away.

Reluctantly I quit spying and headed home through the woods. About halfway through, I felt a low vibration and heard that murmuring sound. I stopped. There it was, the fat, old tree with the hole in it. Voices floated on the wind, whispering words I couldn't catch.

I reached into the hole and felt something. Another note! I unfolded the paper and read it.

Im so stoopid. Im affraid something is rong with my brane. But I dont want anywon to find out or theyll kep me back.

Mom's bell kept ringing *hurry home, hurry home*. I tossed the note back into the tree — somehow it didn't seem right to keep a second secret — and ran the rest of the way through the woods, thinking.

A lot of kids I knew were bad spellers — including both of the Mean Boys. They were always doing dumb things. I wished they *would* be held back a grade, then I wouldn't have to see them so much at school.

Hugo Calderon wasn't the greatest speller, but he wasn't stupid. And he was only eight — learning to spell takes time. Once I heard Mom say Kip Murphy's little sister, Casey, was dyslexic — that was a possibility. There was a kid named Mike on Bailey Street who'd already had to do first grade twice, and he was now in fourth.

When I came out of the woods, Otis and Esmeralda were clopping down the street. "Straaaaaawwww ... berriesforsale!   Straaaaaaawwwww ... berriesforsale!" Otis hollered. He sat on his cart, shaded by a beach umbrella he'd attached to the front, while his horse, Esmeralda, pulled the cart. Every few days, they trotted through the neighborhood, selling strawberries or corn or other fruits and vegetables. If Otis didn't have anything to sell, he'd sharpen people's knives. Mom and Dad said that he was out of another century, the last of his kind. He waved to me as I crossed the street.

Wendy ran out of her house, trailed by her cat, Phoebe, calling, "Otis! Otis, stop!"

"Whoa." Otis tugged on the reins, and Esmeralda stopped in front of Wendy's house.

"You're early," Wendy said. It was true. Otis usually came around in the late afternoon or early evening, and it was only lunchtime.

Mom stood on the front steps of our house and waved. "Hi, Wendy! Hi, Otis!" Then she put her hands on her hips and said in a less friendly tone, "Minty Mortimer, I don't like you running around in the woods by yourself. All sorts of things could happen."

"But this boy —" I started, but then I stopped, remembering how Dad didn't want me chasing strange boys into the woods. And I'd done it anyway. Twice.

"What boy?"

"Nothing. I'm sorry," I said. "I'll be careful."

"Lunch is almost ready. Run over and buy a quart of strawberries." She gave me five dollars.

"Okay." I walked across the lawn to Wendy's yard. She was heading back inside with a pint of strawberries in her hand.

"Will I see you in the parade next week, Minty?" she

asked. Phoebe purred and rubbed her white fur against my legs.

"Yeah," I said. "Paz and I are doing a roller derby routine."

"I was thinking of dyeing Phoebe's hair red, white, and blue and pulling her along in a wagon."

Otis shook his head. "Don't do that to her, Wendy. Cats are easily embarrassed."

Wendy reddened. She was easily embarrassed too. "You're right, Otis. I should spare her the humiliation."

Phoebe ran back to the house as if she knew we were talking about her. Wendy waved good-bye and followed her.

"Minty, your ankle's all furry," Otis said.

I bent down to brush off the cat hair. It stuck to my fingers.

"Give me a horse any day," Otis said. "Wendy tried to talk me into putting a straw hat on Esmeralda, but I know exactly how Esmeralda would feel about that." He patted his horse.

"She's got her bells." I rattled one of the bells on Esmeralda's harness. "That's decoration enough, right? Quart of strawberries, please."

"Here you go." He piled a few extra strawberries on top of a quart and gave it to me. I gave him the five dollars. "And thank you very much."

I paused to pet Esmeralda on the nose and feed her a strawberry. "Something's different about you today, Minty," Otis said. "Did anything happen?"

"Happen?" I wasn't sure what he meant. How did Otis know something was different about me?

"Your aura changed color," he said. "Used to be you had a yellow halo around you, but it's greenish today. Heading toward blue."

"My aura?" I self-consciously felt the cushion of air around my skin. When he talked about the color of an aura that way, I could almost feel it emanating from me like an electric charge. "What does that mean?"

"Hard to say," Otis said. "It's a change. Good or bad, I can't tell."

He clicked his tongue, and Esmeralda started walking. "Straaaaaaaawwwww . . . berriesforsale!"

Interesting. But not very helpful.

I wandered into the garage and looked at the open cardboard box the boy had been going through. He'd taken something from it, I was sure. But what?

I picked through the junk in the box. On the top was a large envelope marked *Minty School*. Inside were extra copies of my fifth-grade school pictures — the small, wallet-size ones you always get too many of. Mom gave the big ones to our relatives and had one framed in the living room. Paz and I exchanged the wallet size with each other, and these were left over. Mom didn't need them, so she left them in the junk box.

Did the boy steal a picture of me? Why would he do that?

With a little shiver, I remembered that Paz's photo ID was stolen the day before. That was an odd coincidence.

If it *was* a coincidence.

Chapter 8
Lightning Bugs in a Jar

"Dad would let me go." Thea kicked the leg of her chair and glared at Mom. I sat quietly eating my chicken, watching and listening and hoping no one noticed I was there.

"No, he wouldn't," Mom said. "And don't bother contradicting me because I already called him at work to discuss it."

Thea wanted to ride her bike up to the 7-Eleven with Melina after dinner, she said. She didn't want Mom to drive her there. And she would not bring back a Slurpee for me.

"The whole thing sounds fishy," Mom said. "I know what kids do in that parking lot. Your father sees the results in the emergency room all the time."

"What?" I asked. "What do they do?"

Mom and Thea ignored me. They always ignored me when they were fighting.

"There's nothing fishy about it," Thea insisted. "I feel like going for a bike ride with Melina, that's all."

"Can I go with you?" I asked.

"No!" Thea snarled. "Does the whole family have to follow me around wherever I go?"

"I just want a Slurpee," I said.

"I'm sorry, honey," Mom said to Thea. "I'm not letting you ride your bike around town in the dark, number one, and two, no daughter of mine is going to spend her summer loitering at the 7-Eleven, of all places."

"You never let me do anything!" Thea shouted. "You can't keep me locked up in this stupid house forever!" She knocked her chair over with a bang and stomped upstairs.

Mom pressed her palms against her eyes. "I can't take this. . . . You'd think she was living in a prison."

I helped myself to Thea's untouched ear of corn. Mom unpalmed her eyes and blinked at me as if she'd just realized I was there. "Do the Calderons really let Melina ride her bike up to the 7-Eleven at night? I thought they were strict."

"They are," I said. "But they don't know half of what goes on." Mr. and Mrs. Calderon worked in Washington and attended a lot of social events at night. Awa kept an eye on the kids, and Melina was supposed to help out now that she was fifteen. But who watched Melina?

"I liked it better when you all were little," Mom said. "It was so much simpler. Thea used to tag along after me and imitate everything I did." Butter dribbled down my chin. Mom wiped it off with a sad, nostalgic smile that got on my nerves. "Don't be in a hurry to grow up, Minty. You may not know it yet, but this is the best time of life."

"Really?" That was depressing. "There's nothing better after this?"

"That's not what I meant," Mom said. "Never mind. I don't know what I meant. Thea's got me all crazy headed."

"May I be excused?"

"Sure, honey."

I put my plate in the dishwasher and grabbed my lightning-bug jar. Being a kid isn't as great as grown-ups seem to think. Grown-ups are constantly bossing you around, for starters. And then there's school, and gym, and homework. Grown-ups forget about having to eat Brussels sprouts because some adult insists you try it, or getting food spit at you by a Mean Boy at lunch, or studying for math tests, or being told over and over and over you can't do something you want to do. At least Mom and Dad get paid for doing their jobs. Nobody pays me to do my homework.

I went out to the backyard to catch lightning bugs. It's kind of sad, how easy they are to catch. They're so trusting. I always feel guilty when I shut them away in my empty peanut butter jar. I make sure to punch plenty of air holes in the lid for them.

Even though I was mad at her, I went up to Thea's room and knocked on her door.

"What?" she snapped.

I opened the door. Thea was lying on her bed, face-down on her pillow. The lights were off.

"Look," I said. "I brought you some lightning bugs."

Thea lifted her head. Her face was all streaky with tears. "I thought you were Mom." She sat up and took the jar of light. It cast a greenish-yellow glow across her face. "Thanks," she said. "Is it okay if I let them go later?"

"Sure," I said. I understood. Lightning bugs can't live long in a jar. They're for keeping a little while, then letting go. You can always catch more another night.

Thea set the jar on her night table. "Are you okay?" I asked.

"Yeah, I'm okay." She wiped her hand across her wet cheek.

"Then why were you crying?"

"You wouldn't understand."

"Sure I would," I said.

"It's just . . . so stupid," she said. "I don't even know why I'm crying. I don't know why I do anything anymore."

"Oh." Ever since she turned fifteen, Thea had been completely baffling. Nothing she said made sense.

"I don't want to hurt anyone," she said. "You know?"

"I don't want to hurt anyone either."

"This isn't about you."

"Then what's it about?"

"I can't tell you."

"Are you in love with someone?" I was just taking a wild guess. In movies, whenever people started crying into their pillows, it was because they were in love.

"No!" She got up, turned on the lights, and wiped her face. "But let me tell you something, Minty — never fall in love. It's like having a stomachache all the time. A good stomachache, but it still hurts."

"A good stomachache?" Did that mean she *was* in love?

She sat at her dresser and started putting on some makeup.

"Going somewhere?" I picked up one of her eye shadows and opened it.

"No. Put that down."

"Then why are you putting on makeup?" I put down the eye shadow and picked up her hairbrush.

"Why are you so nosy?" She snatched the brush away from me. "Don't use that."

"I was just looking at it." I sat on her bed to give her some space. I picked up her cell phone and stared at the screen.

"What are you doing?" she snapped.

I put the phone down. "Nothing. Keeping you company."

"I don't need you to keep me company. Why are you always touching my stuff? It's like you're physically incapable of keeping your hands to yourself."

She could have come into my room and put her finger-prints on everything I owned if she felt like it, and I wouldn't have cared. But she never felt like it.

"I'm not hurting anything," I pointed out.

"Can you just get out of my room please?"

I stood up and started for the door. On the way I stopped by her desk and picked up a purple pen. "Where did you get this?"

Thea groaned and threw open the bedroom door. "Mom!" she yelled down the stairs. "Minty's touching my stuff!"

"I don't want to hear about it!" Mom called.

"Okay, I'm going." I walked into the hall. "Don't forget to let the lightning bugs go."

"I won't." She shut the door.

Downstairs, Mom was doing the dishes. "I'm going to Paz's," I told her.

"Okay," Mom said. "What's Thea up to?"

"Talking crazy talk," I said.

I went outside. Next door, Mr. Gorelick was practicing at his electric organ. "Disco Duck" sounded kind of eerie on the organ at night.

At the Murphys' house, Casey was riding her bike in a pool of light in the driveway, around and around in a circle. I thought about the note I'd found. I knew dyslexic people often had a hard time with spelling and writing.

But I couldn't just go up to Casey and ask her if she'd written that note. It was a secret, after all.

The light was on in Kip's room, and music blasted out the window. His red Mustang was parked on the street, all shiny, since he'd just washed it that day. I waved to Casey and crossed Western Street to the Calderons' house. I knocked at the back door, and Awa let me in.

"Snack?" She offered me a strip of freeze-dried octopus.

"No, thanks — I just had dinner." Some of Awa's snacks were kind of disgusting. Paz never noticed. She was used to eating freeze-dried octopus and salty plums and chicken feet.

Mr. and Mrs. Calderon were sitting in the living room. I hardly ever went into their living room — it was very formal. All the furniture was silky and gilded and easy to make dirty.

"Hello, Mr. and Mrs. Calderon," I said as I passed by. They liked it when kids were very polite.

"Hello, Araminta!" Mr. Calderon waved me into the room. "We haven't seen you in so long. Come in and tell us all about your summer."

I really wanted to go see Paz, but there was no getting out of this. Mrs. Calderon smiled and nodded encouragingly. I stood in front of them, ready to recite an essay on "My Summer Vacation." Talking to Mr. and Mrs. Calderon was like talking to a teacher or an old relative.

"Well, Paz and I are making up a roller-skating rou-tine for the Fourth of July Parade," I reported. "We're practicing some new tricks."

Their faces clouded. They weren't crazy about the roller derby thing. That's why I said "roller skating" instead of "roller derby." They saw through it.

"Do your parents like you to spend so much time roller-skating?" Mrs. Calderon asked.

"Oh, they don't care," I said. "Long as I stay out of their hair. And don't turn out crazy like Thea."

That was the wrong thing to say. "Paz is going to take figure-skating lessons in the fall," Mrs. Calderon told me. "Between that and school, she won't have much time for other things."

"Really? I didn't know that." This was the first I'd heard about figure-skating lessons. "Well, till then we can goof around, right? I mean, that's what summer is for."

Wrong again. "Summer can be just as productive as the rest of the year," Mr. Calderon said. "Why waste pre-cious time?"

I knew they wanted me to say something like *You're right — please excuse me while I go learn calculus*, but I just couldn't. I liked wasting time. I wasn't brave enough to say it to Mr. and Mrs. Calderon, though.

"You may go upstairs and see the girls now," Mr. Calderon said. Dismissed.

"Nice to see you!" I waved and backed out of the room. I almost felt like bowing. I ran up the stairs, glad to get away.

Lennie lay on her bed reading a book called *Man-Bat! The Story of Man-Bat*, and Paz was propped up on her bed texting someone. "Where's Melina?" I asked.

"She's babysitting." Paz didn't look up from her phone. "At Troy's house."

"Ooh. Hope she makes it out alive." Then I realized that she couldn't go to the 7-Eleven with Thea if she was babysitting. Hmm.

I sat on the bed next to Paz. Paz scratched her arm. "What's all this about figure skating?" I asked.

"What?" Paz put her phone away. "Nothing. Mami wants me to take lessons. It doesn't have to be figure skating. It could be ballet. Just some kind of lessons to keep me busy." She scratched her arm again. "Why am I so itchy?"

"But you're already busy," I said. Her phone vibrated on the bed. "Were you texting someone?"

"Just Isabelle." Paz gave a *no big deal* shrug, but she didn't look me in the eye. That's when I noticed the four silver barrettes she was wearing in her hair. Four barrettes all in a row. Last time I saw them, Isabelle, Katie, and Lydia wore three barrettes in their hair. I wondered if they were all wearing four now.

"Did you know that the Man-Bat flies over people's rooftops at night, looking for stray dogs and cats to snack on?" Lennie informed us from across the room.

"Did you know that if you mention the Man-Bat one more time you're going to be his next meal?" Paz said. She scratched again. She seemed very irritable. Her forearm was all red, and little bumps were popping up at an alarming rate.

"Paz, what's wrong with your arm?" I said. "It looks like you have a rash."

Paz rubbed it. "It's so itchy!"

"Don't scratch," I said. "It could get infected."

"I can't help it!" Paz said. "Where did this come from?"

"Are you allergic to anything?" I asked.

"I don't know! Make it stop!" She jumped up off her bed. "Awa!"

Awa came in, trailed by Hugo and Robbie. She looked at the rash, then went into the bathroom down the hall.

"What's going on?" Hugo asked.

"Paz has developed a mysterious rash," Lennie said. She put down her book and sat up, suddenly very interested in Paz's health. "Have you noticed that a lot of weird, bad things have been happening to you lately, Paz? The stomach pains the other day, and then your ID was stolen, and now this mysterious rash —"

"What's your point?" Paz snapped.

"Point?" Lennie said. "I have no point."

"It's like you're cursed," I said.

"Some people say the Man-Bat can curse people," Lennie noted.

The rash was growing redder and itchier by the second. Awa returned with some cream and spread it on Paz's arm.

"It's not a curse," Paz said. "It's just bad luck."

Awa shook her head vigorously. "No, no. Not bad luck. Curse."

"But who would curse Paz?" I asked.

"What about the Witch Lady?" Hugo said.

Paz shuddered at the memory of Halloween night. "That was months ago. Why would she start cursing me now?"

"Witches don't need reasons," Hugo said.

"But that wasn't my fault," Paz said. "I didn't egg her stupid house."

"Yeah, but the Witch Lady doesn't know that," Lennie said. "Remember what she said? 'Curse you kids!' Sounds like a curse to me."

"Maybe she stole your ID to get your picture," Hugo said. "Witches use people's pictures to cast spells on them."

"Who told you that, Hugo?" I asked.

"Otis," Hugo said. "Where he comes from in Louisiana, everybody goes around cursing everybody else all the time."

I thought about the boy in camouflage. Had he stolen my school picture? What would he want with it?

Maybe he would use it to curse me. Maybe he was the Witch Lady's helper!

If she was cooking up curses, it looked like I might be next.

Chapter 9
The Model Home

Early the next morning, I went back to the tree.

Its vibration hummed in my rib cage, calling to me: *Mmmmm . . . Mmmmminty . . .*

I stopped and stared at the hole — a small, dark, mysterious space. I reached inside, feeling around for the last secret I'd left there, the one from the kid who was afraid something was wrong with his or her brain. I touched a slip of paper and pulled it out.

It was a new secret.

I put a curse on my enemy. And it's working.

I read the secret again. I could hardly believe it.

Someone really *was* putting a curse on Paz!

The world seemed to tilt. If Paz could be cursed, anything was possible. Who knew, maybe the Man-Bat was real too.

I couldn't leave the secret in the hole — it was too important. I put it in my pocket and walked home.

Dad was on his way to work. "I just stopped by the Calderons' to check on Paz's rash," he said. The rash had flared all night but was fading by the time Dad looked at it. Just like the stomach pains. Same pattern.

"I told her no swimming for a couple of days, in case the chlorine irritates her skin," Dad said. "But she's fine."

"I'll go over and see her later."

"That's nice." Dad gave me a kiss and drove off to work. I sat on the steps, fingering the secret in my pocket. Dad said Paz was okay. But this slip of paper told a different story.

Pfft pfft pfft pfft . . . David and Troy rode down the street on their bikes. David leaned over and spat. Troy popped a wheelie.

"Hey, loser," David called. I didn't take it personally. David called everybody "loser." I sometimes wondered if it was because he couldn't remember anyone's real name.

Then I saw it: another flash. It came from the edge of the woods. I focused my eyes as hard as I could until I picked out the mystery boy in his camouflage outfit. He pointed his camera at the Mean Boys on their bikes.

The Mean Boys disappeared down Western Street. They hadn't noticed the flash. But I kept my eye on that boy. *Flash!* He took another picture.

"Hey, you!" I shouted. "What are you doing?"

The boy turned and ran through the woods. I chased him. This time I wouldn't just watch him. I was going to catch him and find out what he was up to. Unless he went into the Witch House, of course. In that case, I'd turn around and run screaming in the other direction.

"Stop! I won't hurt you!" I yelled. The boy didn't stop. He ran all the way through the woods. He ran right past the Witch House, past the empty, half-finished houses that surrounded it, down the dusty, unpaved road to the house marked MODEL HOME. He ran inside and shut the door behind him.

I dashed over to the model home and tried the door. It was locked. So I knocked. I rang the doorbell. "I know you're in there!" I called. "You have to come out sometime! I'm going to sit right here and wait until you do."

I couldn't wait forever. If Mom rang the bell, I'd have to go home. But the boy didn't know that.

The ground around the unfinished houses was just mud and straw. The Witch House was gray and peeling and cobwebby, with an overturned couch on the front porch and trash in the yard. A curtain moved in the window. Was someone watching? Or was it just the wind?

The Model Home was the most inviting place in the development, new and clean and surrounded by a carpet of green sod.

I heard a noise from inside the house. I knocked again. "I swear I won't hurt you! I just want to talk to you."

The door swung open, and there he stood. The boy in the camouflage.

He was short, shorter than me, and his hair was yellow fluff like a baby duck's, shorn close to his head. Around his neck hung the chunky, black plastic thing I'd seen on him before.

"Is that a camera?" I asked.

"Yes."

"Did you take my picture with it?"

He didn't answer.

"Did you steal one of my school pictures out of my garage?"

"No."

He was lying. "I know you did," I said. "You can tell me the truth. I won't say anything."

The boy said nothing.

"I know you took something," I said. "I saw you."

"I'll give it back," he said.

Aha!

"That's okay," I told him. "My mom was going to throw it out anyway. But you still shouldn't have taken it without asking."

I thought he was going to say he was sorry, but he didn't.

"Is this your house?" I asked.

"Uh-huh."

"Can I come in?"

"Okay." He stepped aside to let me in. A painting of a farmhouse hung on the wall of the entryway, with a bowl of plastic flowers on a table below it.

"I'm Minty Mortimer," I said.

The boy shook my hand. "Raymond Delmore Junior." He leaned forward and sniffed me. "You don't smell very minty. You smell kind of sweaty. And grassy."

"Yeah, well, they didn't name me for my smell. They named me after my grandmother Araminta."

"My grandmother's name is Kelly," Raymond said. "That rhymes with smelly."

"Yes, it does." *Kelly* rhymed with *smelly* — that was undeniably true. But it had nothing to do with anything that I could see. "I know a dog named Kelly."

Speaking of smells, this house had a strange one. Most houses smell like the people who live in them. I'm used to my own house's smell, so I don't notice it, but Paz says it smells like lemons, pizza, and rubbing alcohol. Mom does disinfect things a lot. The Calderons' house smells like onions and wood polish and Play-Doh. The Gorelicks' house is air freshener, menthol, and pot roast. Everybody's house has a different people smell.

This model home smelled like vinyl, paint, and new carpeting. It had no "people" smell.

Raymond led me into the living room. There was a black leather couch, some stiff-looking chairs, and a Barcalounger with the footrest out. The glass coffee table was littered with comic books, a harmonica, an open can of grape soda, a notebook, glue, tape, scissors, and a pencil.

"So this is really your place?" I asked.

"Sure is."

"Where are your parents?"

"They have their own houses. This house is just for me."

"Wow. How'd you get your own house?"

"The construction workers left it for me," Raymond said. "They left a few weeks ago and they haven't come back. I think they ran out of money." He paused. "So it's my house now."

He plopped down on the Barcalounger, king of the castle. I stayed on my feet. I had something to confront him with and wanted the advantage of height.

I pulled the latest secret out of my pocket — the one about the curse — and waved it in Raymond's face. "What do you know about *this*?"

His eyes lit up. "Another one!" He grabbed the paper and read it, moving his lips slightly.

"Are you putting a curse on my friend?" I demanded.

Instead of answering, Raymond reread the secret.

"Why do you keep taking pictures of us? Are you a spy? Or are you using the pictures to cast a voodoo spell?"

Raymond opened the notebook on the coffee table and held the slip of paper over it.

"Can I have this?" he asked.

This was not the reaction I was expecting. This boy wasn't easily intimidated. "I don't know," I said. "What are you going to do with it? Use it in one of your curses?"

"I'm not cursing anyone," Raymond said.

"How do I know you're not lying?" I asked. "You lied before, about my school picture. For all I know you've got voodoo dolls for everyone in Catonsville."

"I need this." He clutched the scrap of paper. "Please let me keep it."

"What do you need it for?"

He paged through the notebook. There were pictures of people from the neighborhood: Lennie playing kickball, Hugo and Robbie wrestling on the grass, Casey Murphy riding her bike in the driveway, Melina playing her guitar. Raymond added two more pictures to the book: Troy and David on their bikes. The photos he'd just taken.

"You took these pictures?" I asked.

"With this." Raymond touched the blocky camera around his neck. It said POLAROID in small silver letters on one side. "See, you take a picture, and a second later it comes out of this slot." He showed me where the pictures came out. "You don't need a computer or anything. You just wait a few minutes for it to develop itself."

"So why did you steal my school picture?" I asked. "Why not just take one of me with your camera?"

"This camera's old," he explained. "I'm on my last roll of film."

"So? Buy more."

"I don't have any money. Besides, this film is hard to find."

Raymond turned another page. There I was, smiling dorkily in last year's school picture.

"Hey! You *did* steal it."

"I needed it." He closed the book and hugged it to his chest. "For the book."

"What is this book?" I sat down on the couch. "Let me see it."

He clutched the book tighter.

"I promise I won't take it away. I just want to see it."

He hesitated.

"You have to show it to me," I said. "Because my picture's in there."

Raymond set the book on the table. On the cover, in crayon, was written, *My Book of Frends.*

"You spelled *friends* wrong," I pointed out. He picked up a crayon and added an *i.*

I opened the book. Taped to the first page was Paz's missing photo ID.

CHAPTER 10

The Secret Notebook

"You stole this too!" I peeled Paz's photo ID off the page. "From the roller rink! I didn't see you there."

"Nobody saw me," Raymond said. "When I wear my camouflage, I'm practically invisible."

"I can see you just fine."

"That's because I let you see me."

"Okay . . ." I turned another page in the book. A few scraps of paper were slipped between the pages. They were just like the notes I'd found in that murmuring tree. Secrets.

I'm in love with Kip Murphy.

I just want people to like me.

I wish I had the guts to run away.

Im so stoopid. Im affraid something is rong with my brane. But I dont want anywon to find out or theyll kep me back.

"I found this one before." I pointed to the badly spelled note. The others I hadn't seen. "Where did you get them?"

"From the Secret Tree."

So I wasn't the only one. To be sure, I said, "You mean . . . that tree in the woods? With the big hole in it?"

Raymond nodded. "A ghost lives in that tree. He eats secrets."

"A ghost." I blinked. That would have sounded crazier to me than Lennie's stories of the Man-Bat, except . . . I'd felt something. The humming. The murmur.

"People tell secrets to the spirit in the tree, and the spirit makes the secrets go away," Raymond said. "He swallows them and whispers them out on the wind."

"Who told you that?"

"Otis," Raymond said. "He drives down our road once in a while. He gives me some strawberries or a watermelon, if he has extra. He says if I don't take them, he has to throw them away."

"Does he ever talk about your aura?" I asked.

"No," Raymond said. "But he told me about ghosts and spirits, and how they can live in the trees."

"That's just a story," I said. "Like the Man-Bat."

"It's true. One day the construction workers were digging up the dirt under that house there —" Raymond pointed out the window at the unfinished house closest to the woods. "And they found a skeleton. They dug up a grave by accident."

"A grave!" I thought of Crazy Ike, buried long ago on the Witch Lady's farm.

Raymond nodded. "They took the skeleton away and kept on building the house. I told Otis about it, and he said it must have been the bones of Crazy Ike."

"The boy who died from a bat bite!" I knew it.

"Otis said when you disturb a spirit's grave, the ghost floats out of the ground and goes to live in a tree. Especially a tree with a hole in it. And it eats secrets. So if you find a tree with a hole in it, you can put your secret in there, and the spirit makes it go away."

"So Crazy Ike's ghost lives in that tree? I thought Crazy Ike turned into the Man-Bat."

"You believe in the Man-Bat?" Raymond scoffed. "He's not real."

"And Crazy Ike's ghost is?"

"Yes." Raymond said. "I saw him. I saw his spirit float out of the ground and fly into the woods. He lives in that tree. Didn't you feel it humming? That's his spirit. He's calling out, 'Bring me your secrets. . . .'"

"I did feel it humming," I said. "It sounded like voices murmuring."

"Those are the secrets blowing on the wind," Raymond said.

"Oh." This story was crazy, far-fetched . . . but I believed it.

"After they dug up those bones, the construction guys started having problems. One of their trucks broke, some pipes wouldn't work, and the wood they used had termites. They stopped coming to work. Otis said Crazy Ike cursed them."

"Because he was mad that they dug up his grave?"

"Yes. But I think Crazy Ike made sure they left this model house for me to live in. Because Crazy Ike looks out for me."

"How does Otis know so much about spirits?" I asked.

"He's from Louisiana," Raymond told me. "He knows voodoo."

Voodoo! That could not be a coincidence.

"Do you think Otis put a curse on my friend Paz?" I asked.

"I don't think so." Raymond reached for the can of grape soda and tilted it toward his mouth. It was empty. "Why would he?"

"He probably wouldn't." But the Witch Lady would.

I looked at the notebook again. "What about all these secrets? Why didn't the tree eat them?"

"Maybe it was full."

"Raymond —"

"Or maybe I took them out of the hole before the tree had a chance to swallow them."

"But that means those secrets won't go away."

"These are my friends' secrets," Raymond said. "I'm just trying to help them. That's why I made this notebook. I put in pictures of all my friends and try to match the secret to the person. When I've matched them all, I'll put the secrets back in the tree."

"I think you should put them back now," I said. "And stop taking pictures of everybody."

"But don't you want to know who put a curse on your friend?" Raymond asked.

He was right. Paz had already suffered a stomachache and a rash. Something worse — much worse — could be next.

"We'll make a list of suspects," Raymond said. "Then spy on them to find out if they're doing curses."

I knew it wasn't right to spy. But this was a matter of life and death. Possibly. Anyway, it was extremely important.

"Where should we start?" I wanted to start with the Witch Lady, but I was afraid to say so. I hadn't quite figured out what Raymond's relationship with her was, if any. After all, he had his own house. Maybe he had nothing to do with her.

Or maybe he was related to her. And maybe he got touchy when people called her a witch.

"How about those Mean Boys?" Raymond suggested.

"Good idea. They're mean to everybody. But they could have a special grudge against Paz." I suspected Troy of having a crush on Paz. That would be a weird reason to curse someone, but Troy had a twisted mind.

"If they do, we'll find out. And I'll take pictures so we'll have proof."

"Then we can call the police on them and get them arrested," I said.

Raymond paled. "Not the police. We can handle this without them."

"We'll tell my parents, then. And Paz's parents."

"Yeah."

"We'll start tonight," I said. "Meet me at the edge of the woods across from my house, just after dark. And bring your camera."

"I will."

I picked up Paz's ID. "I'm taking this back to Paz."

"No! She'll think you stole it."

"I'll tell her you stole it," I said. "That happens to be the truth."

"No. You can't tell her about me."

"Why not?"

"You can't tell anyone about me. And you especially can't tell anyone about my secret house."

"But why?"

"Because we're spies now," Raymond said.

"But —"

"Promise you won't tell."

"But —"

"Promise. Or I won't help you find out who put a curse on your friend."

I wanted his help. And nothing was more important than saving Paz from the curse.

"Okay," I agreed. "But once the mystery is solved, can I tell?"

"No," Raymond said. "Never."

CHAPTER 11
The First Spy Mission

After dark I climbed down the big tree outside my window and dashed across the front yard, darting behind bushes and cars until I reached the safety of the woods. No one saw me. I waited among the trees, watching the lightning bugs twinkle.

While I waited, my head was full of other people's secrets, especially the new ones.

I'm in love with Kip Murphy.

I just want people to like me.

I wish I had the guts to run away.

Did everyone around me have secrets? These were serious, the last one most of all. In order to want to run away, you'd have to be pretty sad. And it made me sad to think that someone around me was that sad. Like the person who felt like only a goldfish loved him or her. Sadness seemed to be spreading everywhere.

"Minty Mortimer . . ." someone whispered.

"Who's there?" I whirled around. I knew I was meeting Raymond, but he'd startled me.

He stepped out of the shadows in his camouflage outfit and a black ski mask, his boxy camera hanging from his neck. I wore a black T-shirt and jeans to blend into the night.

"Where do we start?" Raymond asked.

"Troy's house." My reason: Thea had said that love hurt like a stomachache. So if Troy had a crush on Paz, his stomach probably hurt. Maybe he thought that a stomachache would make Paz like him back. It was twisted, but that's the Mean Boy Way.

Or maybe Troy just felt like doing something mean to Paz. That was always a possibility.

We crossed through the shadowy gulf between the Murphys' house and Wendy's and into Troy Rogers's backyard. Raymond hesitated at the border.

"They don't have a dog, do they?" he whispered.

I shook my head. "Cat. Named Slayer. He might scratch."

Raymond nodded, and we continued into the yard. A light glowed from the kitchen window at the side of the house. We crept up to it and peeked inside.

Mr. Rogers was washing the dishes and singing along with the radio. He was a chubby man, big like Troy.

Slayer, an orange tomcat, ate from his dish by the sink. He was big and fat too.

"I want to know what love iiiiis!" Mr. Rogers wailed to the music as he slotted the dishes into the dishwasher. Slayer ignored him. I wondered where Troy was. Up to no good, surely.

Mr. Rogers gave me a ride to school every once in a while. The previous fall, for three whole months, his eyes had been red every morning. I didn't think much of it. Maybe he had allergies. Then I realized I hadn't seen Mrs. Rogers around in a long time. Eventually, Mom told me Mrs. Rogers had left them.

"I don't blame her," I'd said at the time. "I wouldn't want to live in the same house with Troy either."

"Araminta Mortimer, that's a heartless thing to say," Mom had told me. "Someday you'll understand."

It turned out that Mr. Rogers had been crying all night long, every night, for three months. But he looked okay now.

Mr. Rogers poured soap into the dishwasher and clicked it shut. Slayer finished eating and licked one of his legs. Mr. Rogers squatted down to pet Slayer, who hissed at him. Mr. Rogers pulled his hand away. Slayer went back to licking his leg.

"Sorry, buddy. I know you're touchy these days. . . ."

Raymond nudged me. "I'm bored," he whispered.

I understood. I waved at him to follow me around to the back of the house.

We crawled along the brick wall until we found another light, coming from the basement. Perfect. Very easy to peek into.

Troy sat on the rec room floor with the TV on, a jar of lightning bugs at his side. A fishbowl sat on top of the TV. Troy's birthday goldfish from Mr. Jack swam a restless figure eight.

Troy removed the lightning bugs from the jar one by one and smashed them on a plate with a plastic hammer. Then he wiped the dead lightning bugs' green glow juice on his face like war paint.

"He's sick," I muttered. "How can he do that to the poor lightning bugs?"

"Maybe that's a voodoo ritual," Raymond suggested.

"Yeah." It was evil, that's for sure. But I saw no dolls of any kind, voodoo or otherwise, in the basement. "It's not proof, but Troy is a suspect."

Something cold and wet bumped my arm. "Whoa!" I jumped and let out a shout.

"Meow!" Slayer rubbed himself against my leg.

"Ssshh!" Raymond clamped his hand over my mouth, too late. Troy looked up toward the window. Raymond and I ducked down. Slayer meowed again, then ran off in the direction of Wendy's house.

"Slayer?" Troy stood up and walked to the window.

"We better get out of here," Raymond whispered. He and I ran around the house and out of the yard until we got to the sidewalk on Carroll Drive. We slowed down and tried to act normal, like we weren't running for our lives from a crazed lightning-bug killer.

We strolled casually down the street. Next door, Mr. Jack's house was lit up and noisy, his driveway full of cars — that could only mean poker night. Next to Mr. Jack was the Carters' house, already decorated for the Fourth of July with red, white, and blue streamers on the porch, red, white, and blue lights along the roof and in the trees, a giant American flag, a plastic Mount Rushmore that played "America the Beautiful," and a life-size, blow-up Uncle Sam in the yard. The Carters overdecorated for every holiday. Easter was the worst, with pastel bunnies and eggs all over the place.

We stopped in front of a squat brick house with lights on in every window and sappy music blaring from the living room.

"David Serrano's house," I told Raymond.

We ran to the side of the house, clinging to the shadows, and peered through the living room window. Mr. and Mrs. Serrano and two of David's three sisters — Claudia and DeeDee — were tangoing cheek to cheek.

The kitchen counter was piled with melons and peaches and bananas — Mr. and Mrs. Serrano own a fruit stand in Lexington Market — around a fish tank with four goldfish in it, one for each of the Serrano kids. But no David.

"David's room is upstairs," I said. The tango music was so loud, there was no need to whisper. "Come on."

An ivy-covered trellis ran up the side of the Serranos' house, right between two second-floor bedrooms: David's and his older sister Connie's.

"You're lighter," I said. "You go."

Raymond scrambled up the trellis like a monkey. He leaned to the left and peered through a window. He leaned to the right and looked into that window. He pointed at the right window.

"What's he doing?"

Raymond climbed down the trellis. "He's not doing anything."

"What do you mean, he's not doing anything? He must be doing *something*."

"Well, he's sitting at his desk. And he's reading."

"Reading? David Serrano?" Impossible. David was in my class last year. He hated reading. "I've got to see this." The trellis strained as I climbed up. There he was, sitting at his desk with headphones on, reading a very fat book — a dictionary or encyclopedia or something like that. I checked the room for signs of evil spells: dolls, pins, herbs . . . but saw nothing suspicious.

Unless you count the fact that he was sitting at his desk, studying, which was very suspicious. It was summer.

School was out. Why would a boy who hated to read be reading unless he had to?

Summer school. If anyone had to go to summer school, it would be David Serrano.

But even if he had to go to summer school, he still wouldn't study.

Unless he was studying voodoo spells!

Out of curiosity, I leaned to the left and looked into Connie's room. She sat at a vanity table, brushing her hair over and over and over. She had dolls all over the place, dozens of dolls . . . but they were all the fancy, dressed-up, collectible kind, not the kind you put pins in.

I climbed down to consult with Raymond. "No hard evidence of voodoo. But David stays on our suspect list."

"Who's next?" Raymond asked.

I wanted to say the Witch Lady. If anyone knew voodoo, it would be her.

But I was afraid to say it to Raymond. I don't know what stopped me, maybe some sense that it would upset him.

There was also the fact that I had no desire to spy on the Witch Lady. What if she caught me? Then *I'd* get cursed.

"What about that lady who lives next door to you?" Raymond asked.

"Wendy? She's nice. I don't think she'd hurt anyone."

"Everyone is a suspect," Raymond said.

"You're right. Let's go."

We walked back up Carroll Drive and turned left on Western Street, approaching Paz's house. A shadow flitted across the back wall.

A bat?

I stopped.

The shadow dropped out a window and bypassed a pool of light by the back door. Someone was sneaking out of Paz's house.

I ducked behind a parked car and pulled Raymond down with me. The shadow slipped out of the Calderons' yard and crossed Western Street. Pink shorts, a tank top, and long, dark hair flashed under the streetlamp. It was Melina.

"Where's she sneaking off to?" I wondered.

"Let's follow her," Raymond said.

Melina stopped outside the Murphys' house, just across Western Street from her own. She beamed up at a window on the second story like she was wishing on a star. Then she ducked into a shrub to hide. I waited. She didn't move. It was as if she'd disappeared.

"That's funny," Raymond said. "We're out spying, and so is she. The world is full of spies."

"Kip," I said. "She must be waiting for Kip."

Kip Murphy's Mustang wasn't in the driveway, and his bedroom light wasn't on.

"Why?" Raymond asked.

"She likes him. Don't you see? We've just solved one of the secrets. 'I'm in love with Kip Murphy' must be Melina's secret."

"Yeah," Raymond said. "When I get home I'll paste that one under her picture."

There was a roar down the street and a flash of headlights. Kip's Mustang squealed into the driveway. He gunned the engine. Melina stepped out of the bushes and straightened her tank top. She gave her hair a quick brush with her hands to make sure there were no leaves in it. Then she started walking down the sidewalk toward the Murphys' driveway, like she was just passing by, la-di-da-di-da.

Kip got out of the car. "Hey, Melina."

"Kip! I was just out for a walk. Where are you coming from?"

"Nowhere special. Stopped at the 7-Eleven."

"See anybody there?"

"Not really. See you later."

"Bye, Kip."

Kip jogged up the four steps to his front door and disappeared inside his house. Melina walked slowly, watching him all the way. The porch light went out. The light in Kip's room went on. She lingered on the corner a few seconds longer. Then she crossed the street and sneaked back into her own house.

"I should go home too," I said. Sometimes my parents

checked on me while I was sleeping. I'd left a bunch of pillows under my covers to suggest a body, but if they turned on the light, they'd know I was gone, and I didn't need the drama.

"But we haven't solved the voodoo mystery yet," Raymond said. "Can you come over tomorrow?"

"I'm supposed to go roller-skating tomorrow with Paz. We're practicing a routine for the Fourth of July Parade."

"How about the day after?"

"Okay. We'll meet the day after tomorrow to plan another spy mission. I just hope the curse doesn't kill Paz before then."

We shook hands on it. Raymond slipped off into the woods like a shadow. I went home and crawled into bed, undetected.

Chapter 12
Missing!

"Minty Fresh dodges a block by Pax A. Punch! She pulls ahead for the win!" I ducked under Paz's flailing arm and raced past her on my skates.

"I wasn't really trying." Paz rolled listlessly toward a bench on the sidelines of the track.

Paz was not putting much energy into our routine. It was like she didn't even care about roller derby anymore.

"Paz, we've got to practice. The parade is next week. If we don't have a roller-skating routine, we'll have to decorate our bikes and ride with Lennie and Hugo, and that's so babyish."

"The whole parade is babyish," Paz said. "That's what Isabelle says. She hasn't even gone to the parade since she was six."

"Isabelle." I crossed my arms. "Of course *Isabelle* would say that."

"What do you mean?"

"Nothing."

"We'll be in middle school next year," Paz said. "We've got to think about our reputations. Are we going to be cool girls with lots of friends? Or are we going to be dorks who roller skate in a baby parade?"

"Roller derby is cool," I said.

"To you, maybe."

"So you don't want to do roller derby anymore?" Paz and I had been planning our derby auditions since we were eight. We'd been lobbying the Oella Roller Rink to start a junior team all year. Now Paz didn't like it anymore?

What else didn't she like?

"You can't quit roller derby," I said. "You've got the perfect name! Pax A. Punch!" I loved saying it out loud.

"You can have it," Paz said. "You can be Pax A. Punch."

"But my name isn't Paz," I said. "Don't you get it? It doesn't work. The joke's not funny unless your name is Paz."

"Change your name to Paz, then." She untied one skate, then paused to rub her nose. "My nose is all tickly. I don't know if I'm getting a cold or what."

Maybe she was getting a cold. Or maybe the curse had struck again.

I tried not to get mad at Paz. I imagined how it would feel to be cursed. If I was always getting rashes and stomachaches and a tickly nose, I'd be cranky too.

"So no more practice?" I asked. "We're not going to skate in the parade together?"

"You can do it by yourself if you want to," Paz said. She adjusted her barrettes. She always wore four silver barrettes in a row now. "I bet Lennie would skate with you if you asked her."

So now Paz was trying to pawn me off on her little sister? The fact that Lennie wanted to skate just proved that it was babyish.

The weird thing was, I still wanted to skate in the parade, even if it *was* babyish. I'd always been in the parade, ever since I was little. Mom used to pull me and Thea down the street in a decorated wagon. Later I tagged after Thea on my tricycle. Then Paz and I wrapped our bikes in patriotic streamers and rode down Carroll Drive with all the other kids.

Why stop now? I wasn't ready. What would I do with myself if I wasn't in the parade? Just stand on the sidewalk and watch? That seemed so . . . boring.

Then I remembered something awful.

"What about my birthday party?" I asked Paz.

"What about it?"

I was turning eleven on August 27 and had planned a roller-skating party — with a roller derby theme — at the rink. Which Paz knew perfectly well.

Paz had turned eleven in May. Her birthday party's theme was "April Showers Bring May Flowers." I'd thought it was strange at the time — not very Pax A. Punchy — and figured her mother had forced her to have a flower party. But maybe it had been a warning signal. Maybe I should have paid attention.

"My mom already booked the rink for that afternoon," I reminded her.

"Who wants to go roller skating in August?" Paz said. "If I had a summer birthday, I would definitely have a pool party."

"But I don't have a pool," I objected. "And neither do you."

"At Rollingwood, silly. You can reserve a barbecue and have it at night, with a DJ and dancing and everything. We could buy new bathing suits for the party!"

"I guess that would be fun," I said.

"Tell your mom you want to change it," Paz said. "You've got time."

"Okay," I said. "So we're not skating anymore?"

"No," Paz said. "Let's go home."

I took off my skates, and we walked back to Woodlawn Road. There was a commotion outside Wendy's house. Lennie, Hugo, Casey, and Kip circled Wendy, who was crying.

"Phoebe is gone!" Wendy sobbed. "She never runs away. Someone must have stolen her!"

"We already made a sweep through the neighborhood," Kip told me.

"We couldn't find her anywhere," Hugo said.

"But we did find this clue." Lennie held up a tuft of white fur. "Snagged on that holly branch there." She pointed to a bush in Wendy's backyard.

"What will I do without Phoebe?" Wendy cried. "The house is so lonely without her."

"Don't worry, we'll find her," Kip said.

"A lot of things have been stolen around here lately," Paz said. "Like my photo ID."

Gulp. I hadn't figured out how to give it back to her without breaking my promise to Raymond. She didn't need it anymore, anyway. The rink manager had given her a new one.

"I heard someone in our garage one night last week," Kip reported. "He ran off before I could see him, but he left a box open. There were old pictures scattered all over the garage floor."

Raymond strikes again.

"And there was that flash in the woods!" Lennie said. "A week or so ago, remember?"

That was Raymond too. But he wouldn't have stolen Phoebe. Why would he want a cat? Unless . . .

. . . unless the Witch Lady wanted the cat for a curse. And Raymond was working to help her.

"What about the Man-Bat?" Lennie said. "He eats cats!"

Wendy's face went gray.

"Shh! You dope!" Paz kicked Lennie in the shin. "There's no such thing as a Man-Bat."

"That's what you say," Lennie said.

"We'll find Phoebe," I said. "Don't worry, Wendy."

Raymond had stolen some things. But he wouldn't kidnap a cat.

Would he?

CHAPTER 13
The Snooping Babysitter

The next day, I took the first secret I'd found, the one about the goldfish, out of my treasure box. I'd decided to add it to Raymond's book. When we figured out who it belonged to, we could paste it under that person's picture.

On my way to Raymond's model home, I stopped by the Secret Tree and found a new slip of paper:

When I'm babysitting, after the kids are asleep, I snoop through the parents' drawers and closets.

Interesting. Both Melina and Thea babysat. There were other babysitters in the neighborhood too, like Isabelle's older brother, Martin, and old Mrs. Humm, who used to sit for me and Thea. She was so old I was afraid she'd die at our house, and then what would we do? "It's worse than having no sitter at all!" Thea complained, but Mom and Dad still hired Mrs. Humm. They liked a "more mature" sitter.

I could imagine Thea snooping. But who was I to judge? I was fast becoming the neighborhood spy.

Thea and I were alike that way. Nosy. I was curious about how other people lived. What was it like to be older than me, to be a teenager or an adult? It was like peeking into my own future.

And now I was finding these secrets that showed me what was going on in people's hearts — if only I could figure out whose secrets they were.

I brought the new secret to Raymond's house and pressed the doorbell. It chimed a formal tune, like church bells: *ding-dong ding-dong* . . .

Raymond peeked at me through the window, then let me in. I immediately scanned the house for signs of Phoebe — white fur, traces of kitty litter, that certain cat smell. But instead of cat, I was beginning to notice a new smell in the house. A Raymond smell: peanut butter, paper, glue, and Dr Pepper, with a touch of mud.

I pulled the notes out of my pocket. "I've got one to add to your collection. And I found a new one."

Raymond read the secrets, then opened his notebook. *I'm in love with Kip Murphy* was taped under a Polaroid picture of Melina. Next to that — a school picture of Kip. (What, I wondered, was Kip's secret?)

"Who do you think is the snooping babysitter?" Raymond asked.

"I can think of four possibilities," I said. "One: Mrs. Humm. But she's an old lady and I think she's retired from babysitting. Two: Martin Barton, Isabelle's brother. He lives all the way up at the top of Carroll Drive."

"Okay." Raymond was writing these names down in his book. "Who else?"

"Melina and Thea," I said. "Thea is babysitting for the Carters tonight."

"We'll catch her snooping!" Raymond said.

"Yes, snooping." I opened the refrigerator, snooping myself. Nothing inside but a can of Dr Pepper and a package of bologna. I opened a cupboard. No cat food. "Where's the bathroom?"

"Right here." Raymond opened a door off the kitchen.

I started up the stairs. "I want to use an upstairs one. More privacy."

"Um — okay." He followed me up the stairs.

"There's no privacy if you come with me."

"I'll show you where it is. Then I'll give you the tour."

"Oh. Okay."

He led me through a large master bedroom to a fancy bathroom with a big, round tub. "I'll wait in my room," he said.

"Which one's your room?" I asked.

"The one with the boats."

I shut the door and ran the water in the sink, pretending

to pee. When enough time had passed, I came out. I looked in the closet. It was so big it could have been another bedroom. Phoebe wasn't in there. I checked the king-size bed for cat hair, but it was clean. Then I sat on the bed.

The bed was hard. Very hard.

So hard it had sharp corners.

Raymond came in. I looked under the bedcover. It wasn't a real bed. It was nothing but a wooden platform disguised with a cover and some pillows. "Do you sleep on this thing?"

"It's just for show. The rug is more comfortable." He patted the wall-to-wall carpeting.

"Oh."

"This is a model home. So people can see what the other houses will look like when they finish building them."

"Like an example," I said.

Raymond nodded. "I don't think they'll ever finish, though. Come on, I'll show you the rest."

Raymond's room was painted blue, with bunk beds and pictures of boats on the walls.

"Why didn't you take the big room?" I asked.

"That one's for parents. I took the boy's room. You can have the other one if you want." He led me into a third bedroom, with pink walls and a canopy bed — a total cliché of a girl's room. But I did like the window seat.

"Can I cover up the pink with roller derby posters?" I asked.

"Whatever you want. It's your room."

"Okay, I'll take it." I sat on the canopy bed, but it was just as hard and wooden as the master bed. The window seat had a good view of the second floor of the Witch House. I'd never seen it from this angle before. One pane in the attic window was broken. A shutter hung off its hinge, and some of the roof tiles were missing. It looked dark and dirty and uncared for.

On a line at the side of the house, some clothes were hung to dry: a pair of women's jeans, two women's blouses, plus some Raymond-size T-shirts and a pair of boys' underpants.

Something white flashed in an attic window, just for a second. My muscles tensed. "Was that a cat?"

"Was what a cat?" Raymond asked.

But the white thing was gone.

"Wendy's cat is missing," I told him. "I thought maybe I saw her in the window over . . . there."

Raymond came to the window and looked out. "There's no cat over there."

"How do you know?"

"Because I . . . go there, sometimes."

Aha! So he was connected to the Witch Lady some-how. "You go there?"

He caught me noticing the laundry on the line. "She washes my clothes for me. But I live here."

"No, you don't," I said. "No one lives here."

"*I* do. There's a washing machine in the basement of this house, but it isn't hooked up." He had a pained look on his face, as if he'd just bumped his funny bone.

"Who is she?" I asked. "The lady who lives there?"

Now Raymond looked wary. "Just a lady. Let's talk about something else." He turned his back to the window. "We could have a sleepover here. You sleep in your room, and I'll sleep in mine."

"But . . . the beds aren't real."

"That's okay. We can use sleeping bags on the floor. Do you have a sleeping bag?"

"Yes."

"Do you have an extra one for me?"

"You can use my sister's. Except I don't think my mother will let me sleep over here."

"Tell her you're sleeping at Paz's. Then sneak over here."

"Yeah. Okay. One of these nights." Like I was going to spend the night on this side of the woods — home of the Witch Lady and possibly the Man-Bat — in a pretend house.

"We have to plan tonight's spy mission." We went downstairs because Raymond said he could think better down there. He sat in the Barcalounger and flipped the footrest out. He leaned back, said, "Ahhh," then flipped the footrest back in. He flipped it out again, then in again. "Ahhh."

"Stop that. It's very irritating."

"Sorry." He picked up the harmonica and started playing a song. After a few bars, I recognized "On Top of Old Smoky."

"That's pretty good," I said when he was finished.

"Bring your harmonica over next time and we can play together."

"I don't have a harmonica."

"Too bad," Raymond said. "Everybody needs a harmonica. It's like a little pocket friend. Goes wherever you go."

"I guess."

He played "You Are My Sunshine." It sounded very pretty.

"Maybe I'll ask for a harmonica for my birthday," I said. "I'm turning eleven in August."

"It's only June," Raymond said. "August is way far away."

"Today is July first," I told him. "August is only one month away."

"A month is still a long time." He turned around upside down on the Barcalounger, laying his head on the footrest and his feet on the headrest, and started playing "Frère Jacques."

"Are you having a birthday party?" he asked. "When you turn eleven?"

"Yeah — a roller-skating party. At the roller rink. Do you want to come?"

"I'm not allowed to go to the roller rink," he said.

"Why not?"

"Someone might see me there."

"But you were there the other day, when you stole Paz's ID," I pointed out.

"Sure — in my camouflage. You said yourself you didn't see me. But I can't go there as an official person who roller-skates. I'm hiding out."

"Hiding out from who?"

"It's a secret." He played "Frère Jacques" again. "'Frère Jacques' sounds good when two people play it, like a round. I wish you had a harmonica."

"Even if I did, I don't know how to play."

"I'll teach you."

"You can tell me your secret," I said. "I won't tell anyone."

Instead of answering, he played "Row, Row, Row Your Boat." When he was done, he said, "We better plan the spy mission."

"Okay." I gave up trying to get his secret out of him — for the time being. "Thea is going over to the Carters' house at seven. But it doesn't get dark until around nine. My bedtime is nine thirty, and I have to be in my room when my parents come in to say good night. After that I can sneak out." I hesitated. "Can you meet me outside the Carters' house at ten?" Ten was awfully late.

Raymond said, "I can meet you at midnight if you want."

"Ten's good," I said. "While we're out, we can look for Wendy's cat too."

"Okay."

I watched his face carefully for any telltale twitch of guilt at the word *cat*, but he betrayed nothing. Either he was innocent or he was the world's best liar. Or a combination of both.

CHAPTER 14
Caught!

That night, Raymond wore his usual camouflage. I dressed in black with a black ski mask to cover my face. It was hard to hide in the Carters' front yard, with all the blinking red, white, and blue lights, though the plastic, musical Mount Rushmore gave pretty good cover. Raymond and I played it safe and approached the house from the back.

It was after ten, so Tessie and Bo Carter were asleep. A light glowed from a side kitchen window. I took a peek. The kitchen was clean and empty.

Next, the family room, with the flickering gray-blue light of the TV. Thea sat on the couch, watching TV and eating ice cream out of the carton.

"She's getting her germs in their ice cream!" I whispered. "I bet the Carters would be shocked to know that."

"Should I take a picture of it?" Raymond lifted his Polaroid camera.

"Not yet." Eating ice cream out of the carton wasn't the secret we were looking for. We had to catch Thea in the act of snooping.

We crouched by the window and waited.

Finally, Thea got up. She went into the kitchen. She put the ice cream away. Then she went back to the family room and watched some more TV.

"When are the parents coming home?" Raymond asked.

"I don't know. Late, I guess."

As time passed and Thea did nothing but watch TV, Raymond got restless. Watching Thea watch TV was very boring. We couldn't even see the show from where we stood.

"I have to pee," Raymond whispered.

"So?"

"I really have to pee."

"I repeat: So?"

"So I'm going to go pee by that tree over there."

"No! That's not fair."

"Why not?"

"Someone might see you."

"Someone might see us spying too. Which is worse?"

"I have to pee too."

"So pee."

"No — I can't. Don't you get it? I'm a girl. I can't just go pee on a tree."

"Why not?"

"It's biology, stupid."

"So what's that got to do with me?"

"If I can't pee, you can't pee."

"What? That's not fair."

"No — what's not fair is if you get to pee and I don't."

"I don't care what you say — I'm going to pee."

Raymond wandered off toward the big tree in the backyard. I heard the sound of him peeing. It annoyed me greatly.

There was movement in the family room. Thea got up. She walked down the hall toward the bedrooms.

The Carters' house was just one story and a basement, so spying was easy.

"Raymond!" I whisper-shouted. "The mark is on the move!"

"Just a minute!" He was still peeing. He hadn't been lying when he'd said he really had to go.

I slid along the Carters' brick wall toward the bedrooms, clinging to the shadows. A light went on at the other end of the house.

"Raymond! Hurry!"

Raymond ran up to the lit window. "Which room is that?"

"I think it's the parents' room."

The window was a little too high for me to see into. "I need a boost," I said. "Lift me up so I can see what she's doing."

"You're bigger than me," Raymond said. "Why don't you lift *me* up?"

"She's my sister. You lift me."

I tugged on my ski mask in case Thea happened to look my way. I didn't want her to recognize me. Raymond wove his fingers together to give me a boost. I leaned on his shoulder and stepped on his hands. With a grunt he tried to lift me up.

"Oof! You're heavy."

"I'm not so heavy," I said. "You're weak."

I gripped the crumbly brick windowsill and peered into the room. Thea was sitting on a large double bed. But she wasn't snooping — yet. She was flipping through a magazine.

"What's she doing?" Raymond asked. I could hear the strain of holding me in his voice.

"Reading a magazine."

"Can I put you down now?"

"No!"

But his hands buckled, and I fell. My arms flailed, accidentally knocking against the window. For a split second my ski-masked face pressed against the glass. Thea looked up — and saw me.

She screamed.

I tumbled to the ground. "Run!"

Raymond and I scrambled out of the yard. We didn't stop until we were well into the woods.

CHAPTER 15
The Man-Bat!

I climbed up the tree and sneaked back into my room before Mom burst in, all upset, to check on me.

"Minty? Are you awake?"

"Wh-what?" I sat up and rubbed my eyes as if I'd been asleep.

"Is everything okay in here?" Mom asked.

"Sure. Why? What's going on?"

"Didn't you hear Thea screaming a few minutes ago? Your father and I could hear it all the way from the Carters'."

Ulp. "Screaming? Well, your room faces that way, and mine faces the front. . . ." I heard myself yammering and realized that I was raving like a guilty person. "What happened?"

"Your father is over at the Carters' with her now. Seems she saw a robber's face in the window."

"A robber? What did she look like?"

"She?"

"I mean he. He or she. How would I know?"

"He was wearing a mask, so Thea couldn't see his face. I suppose it could have been a she. . . . Thea's screaming scared him away. Your father just called to let me know everything is all right." She crossed the room and closed my window. "I know it's cool tonight, but we'll put the AC on. I can't sleep knowing someone might try to crawl in!"

I felt bad about upsetting everybody so much. But I didn't realize how truly scared everyone was until the next day.

"It was the Man-Bat," Lennie said. "It's got to be. Fits the description perfectly."

I was hanging out in the Calderons' basement with Lennie, Paz, Melina, and Thea. Melina idly strummed her guitar and kept an eye on Hugo and Robbie, who were building a LEGO fort.

"It didn't look like a bat," Thea said. "It looked like a person."

"That's what the Man-Bat looks like," Lennie said. "A man's head and body with bat wings! Covered in slime. Maybe you didn't see the wings, but they were there. Pressing against windows is totally his thing!"

Lennie shuddered. I shuddered too. I suspect we shuddered for different reasons.

"No more open windows for me," Lennie added. "It's

AC for the rest of the summer. Now that we know for sure that he's out there. . . ."

"We don't know anything for sure," Paz scoffed. "Maybe it was just a kid playing a trick on Thea. It could have been one of the Mean Boys."

"Yeah," I said. "Scaring babysitters is just like something Troy and David would do."

"What about all the things gone missing lately?" Paz said. "Like my ID, and Kip's pictures, and Wendy's cat . . . I think there's a prowler in the neighborhood."

"A prowler?" I said. "You've been watching too many late-night movies, heh-heh, heh-heh."

Paz gave me a long, suspicious squint. I couldn't meet her eye.

"You guys, listen to my new song." Melina strummed her guitar and sang to a poppy beat:

"Hey hey, what a day, it's summer all the way.
Come here, have no fear, it's the best time of the year.
Don't cry, tell me why, see the sun up in the sky, yo.
Summertime's the best time, summertime's the best,
Whoa whoa whoa whoa . . ."

She stood up and danced around with her guitar, singing "Whoa whoa whoa whoa" over and over again. I looked at Paz, and Paz looked at me. She rolled her eyes. That was the signal.

We jumped up and started dancing around like Melina, singing "Whoa whoa whoa whoa!" louder and louder and crazier and crazier. Then Lennie, Hugo, and Robbie joined in.

"Stop it, you guys!" Melina stopped playing, but we all kept singing and dancing until Awa called down from upstairs, "Paz! Telephone!"

Melina's face was red. Thea put her arm around Melina's shoulders. "Siblings. I feel your pain."

"Paz!" Awa called again.

"That's Isabelle." Paz leaped for the stairs and stepped barefoot on a LEGO. "Ow!" She hopped off the pointy block, then kicked the leg of the couch, then tripped over a whole pile of LEGOs —

"Ouch!" She tumbled to the floor, clutching her ankle. "My foot! I stepped on it funny —" She grimaced in pain. "I think I pulled something."

"Let me see." Thea took Paz's foot in her hands and moved it. "Does that hurt?"

Paz screeched. "Ow! Yes! That hurts!"

"We better get Dad," Thea said.

I ran down the street to Mortimer Mansion. Luckily, Dad was off that afternoon. I told him what had happened and brought him back to the Calderons' house. Paz was lying on the floor while Awa held an ice pack to her ankle.

"Never fear, Dr. M is here." Dad always joked when people got hurt so they wouldn't worry. "Let's take a look."

He removed the ice pack and tested Paz's foot and ankle. Her ankle was swollen now. "Looks like you've got a sprain," Dad said. "Not too bad. Nothing broken or anything like that. I'll get my gauze and wrap it up for you. You'll be limping for a while, Paz. Maybe a few weeks."

"What about the Fourth of July Parade?" I asked. I was still hoping Paz would change her mind and roller-skate in the parade with me. But it was only two days away.

"No roller-skating," Dad said. "If someone wants to tow her in a wagon, that's okay."

"What?" Paz said. "I'm not riding around in a wagon. I'd rather just watch."

"That's the smart thing to do," Dad said. He helped Paz upstairs to her room and ordered her to keep her swollen foot iced and elevated as much as possible.

"I've had so much bad luck lately," Paz complained. "First that mysterious stomachache, then my ID gets stolen, that rash . . . and the other day my nose itched like crazy. Now this. Why are all these bad things happening to me?"

"Curse of the Man-Bat," Lennie said.

I couldn't disagree. The curse was working — and getting worse.

Chapter 16
A Present from Raymond

I asked Mom if I could change my birthday party from roller-skating to a pool barbecue. "Paz's ankle's all swollen," I said. "She might not even be able to skate at my party! And then what's the point?"

"You want to change now?" Mom looked annoyed. "But we've already put a deposit on the roller rink for that day. *Nonrefundable.*" She hugged me, but I kept my arms stiff at my side and didn't hug back. I didn't feel like being hugged. "Don't worry, I'm sure Paz's ankle will be better by then. And if it's not, she can still have fun at the party."

"How? How can she have fun at a roller-skating party if she can't roller-skate?"

"Well, she can eat pizza and cake. . . ."

"Big deal." I pouted. "A roller-skating party is babyish anyway. Eleven is too old for that."

"Since when? You love roller skating. I thought you were going to do a whole derby thing."

"I was, but —" I didn't feel like talking about it anymore. "So we definitely can't switch?"

"I'm sorry, honey. You can have a pool party next year if you want."

Next year, when I turned twelve. Who knew what kind of person I'd be by then? Who knew if Paz and I would even be friends next year?

If I had a babyish birthday party that Paz hated, we might not be friends by the end of the summer. I just had that feeling.

"Here's today's secret." I showed Raymond what I'd found in the Secret Tree on my way to visit him. "It's a weird one."

I'm secretly sabotaging my dad's diet shake by putting cream and sugar in it. He keeps saying he can't believe a diet shake could taste so good! And wondering why he isn't losing weight. But I don't want him to. I have my reasons.

"Diabolical," Raymond said. "Who's got a fat father?"

I consulted the secret notebook. By this time, Raymond had pictures of just about everyone in the neighborhood. He must have sneaked off and taken pictures when I wasn't around. "There are five dads who could be on a diet: Mr. Jack, Mr. Rogers, Mr. Serrano, Mr. Kendall, and Mr. Murphy."

"Mr. Jack has a very big belly," Raymond noted.

"Huge," I agreed. "But his kids are grown up. They don't live in the neighborhood anymore."

"Do they come back and visit?"

"Sometimes," I said. "But if they don't live with him, how can they sabotage his diet shake?"

"Good point. Next."

"Mr. Rogers and Mr. Murphy are pretty chubby too. I've seen Mr. Kendall buying diet soda at the grocery store." Mr. Kendall was Lydia's father. "And David Serrano's dad is on the tubby side. Plus he's always yelling at David about being slow. I could picture David sabotaging his diet out of sheer meanness. Or revenge."

"Let's spy on the Murphys tonight," Raymond suggested. "We've already spied on the Rogerses and the Serranos."

"Okay," I said. "But we've got to be careful. Everybody's freaked out about a prowler on the loose. We can't get caught."

"We won't." Raymond took out his harmonica and started playing a song. Then he suddenly stopped. "Hey — I've got a present for you."

"A present for me?" I couldn't imagine what it could be. As far as I could tell, Raymond didn't have any money. "What is it?"

He handed me a small package wrapped in a page from the comics. FOR MINTY was written across it. FROM YOUR BEST FRIEND, RAYMOND.

I paused. I did not consider Raymond to be my best friend. But what could I say? He was giving me a present.

"Open it," he urged.

I unwrapped the package. Inside was a shiny silver harmonica.

"So we can play duets together," he said.

I put the harmonica to my lips and blew a note. It sounded froggy and sweet and wonderful.

"Thank you, Raymond."

"Do you like it?"

"I love it!"

He showed me how to play a scale, how to make different notes by blowing in and out on the same hole, and how to use my fingers to block out the notes I didn't want to play. Then he taught me "Frère Jacques." Soon we were playing it in a round. It sounded very good.

We started with the kitchen, since that's where diet sabotage was most likely to happen. I wore all black and my ski mask. Raymond wore camo as usual.

We tiptoed into the Murphys' yard. Their kitchen was in the back, so we started to round the side of the house. Suddenly, Raymond froze.

"What?" I whispered. "Come on!"

"Someone else is here," Raymond murmured. "Look."

In the shadows under the bushes that lined the side

of the house, something moved. Was it a dog? Was it a prowler? Was it . . . the Man-Bat?

I could just make out a dark head peering into the dimly lit basement window. Someone else was spying on the Murphys!

But who? And why?

"Hide!" Raymond whispered.

We crouched behind the hedge that separated the Murphys' house from Wendy's, very quiet and still, spying on the spy. The crickets and cicadas chirped in the woods. A car rushed down Rockwell Avenue a block away. Waves of laughter came from Wendy's TV.

And somewhere, someone was crying. I strained to pick out the source of the crying from all the other night noises.

It came from the spy. The mystery spy was crying.

From inside the house a face darkened the basement window. "Hey! Is someone out there?"

"That's Kip," I whispered.

The spy jumped up and ran away, sobbing. The shadowy figure crossed the street and ran to the Calderons' house. Pink shorts, a tank top, long, dark hair.

Melina.

The Murphys' back door slammed, and Kip ran around to the side of the house. "Who's out here? What was that noise?" He shined a flashlight all around the yard.

I gripped Raymond's hand, which was very sweaty, squeezed my eyes shut, and held my breath. If Kip found us, he'd think *we* were the ones who were spying on him. Which we would have been, if Melina hadn't gotten there first. But that wasn't the point.

"If you're a prowler, you're in big trouble," Kip shouted. "One more sound and I'm calling the police."

I flattened myself on the grass as flat as I could go, trying to melt into the earth. *Please don't catch us, please don't catch us. . . .*

After more yelling and looking around, Kip finally went back inside the house. I let out my breath.

"We'd better get out of here," I said. "It's too dangerous to spy tonight. Everybody's all edgy."

"But we didn't find out about the diet sabotage," Raymond said.

"Maybe tomorrow night. I don't want to get caught."

Raymond disappeared into the woods. I sneaked back into my room. When I was safely in bed, I took out my harmonica and played it softly. I wondered about Melina. Why was she spying on Kip? Was that what you did when you loved someone?

And what had she seen in his basement that made her cry?

CHAPTER 17
The Neighborhood Prowler

"Did you hear there was a prowler at the Murphys' last night?" Mr. Rogers said. "And I had my windows wide open!"

After dinner on July 3, Mom and I went to a neighborhood meeting at Wendy's house to plan the Fourth of July Parade. Wendy served iced tea and watermelon on her back patio. Almost everybody was there: Troy Rogers and his dad, David Serrano with his mother and sisters, Mr. Jack, Mr. Gorelick and Mrs. Gorelick. . . .

"Another prowler! What is going on around here?" Mr. Jack hoisted his beer. He drank a lot of beer and had the belly to show for it. I had the feeling he wasn't on a diet.

"First the Carters, and now the Murphys." Mrs. Serrano shook her head. "Tsk tsk . . ."

"I wonder if the prowler stole my Phoebe?" Wendy sniffled.

Mr. Rogers touched her arm. "Are you all right here all by yourself at night, Wendy?"

Wendy shook her head. "I don't know. I miss Phoebe. She wasn't useful like a watchdog, but it was nice to have company."

No one loves me except my goldfish, I found myself thinking.

"I know exactly how you feel," Mr. Rogers said.

No one loves me except my goldfish, I thought again.

Troy reached for a slice of watermelon and took a bite. Then he spit three seeds — *pow pow pow* — onto the grass. Like he was shooting at something.

David copied him, spitting watermelon seeds at his sisters. One landed in Connie's ear. "Bull's-eye!" David crowed.

Connie picked the seed out of her ear and threw it back at him. "You don't spit food at people. Don't you know anything?" She turned to Wendy and added, "I don't know if it's a head injury or *what*, but David's never quite been, you know, like the rest of us Serranos."

David took a defiant, embarrassed bite of watermelon and chewed loudly. Wendy's eyes ran down the line of Serrano sisters, from Connie to DeeDee to Claudia. "You mean, because he's not a girl?"

Connie laughed. "No, I mean he's always doing some crazy, stupid thing like setting ants on fire or wearing his underwear outside of his pants."

Pfft! David splattered her with seeds.

"See? Like that!" Connie delicately picked the seeds off her dress.

"That time I put my underwear on over my pants?" David said. "That happened once. In kindergarten. But you won't let me forget it."

"That's because you're always acting like you're still in kindergarten."

"Kids! Quiet!" Mrs. Serrano snapped.

"Maybe we should cancel the parade," Mr. Murphy said.

"Yes! What if the prowler robs our houses while our backs are turned?" Mrs. Serrano said. "We'll all be lined up along Carroll Drive, watching the parade. No one will be home!"

"You think he'll strike in the middle of the day?" Mom said.

"Why not in the middle of the day?" Mrs. Serrano said. "This nut has no fear!"

"Lennie Calderon told me somebody was spying on the kids a few weeks ago, taking pictures and prowling around in the woods," Mrs. Gorelick said. She held Kelly, her wheezy little Pekingese dog, in her arms, rocking her like a baby.

I got chills as they talked. I knew there was no prowler. It was all me and Raymond. If only they knew that the prowler they were so scared of was just a couple of kids! I needed to throw them off our scent.

"The Man-Bat," I said.

"The what?" Everyone turned to look at me.

"Lennie thinks we're being stalked by a monstrous creature who's half-man, half-bat," I explained.

"You mean Batman?" Mr. Rogers asked.

"No. The Man-Bat is more slimy and gross, like a real bat," I said. "Only human-size."

Mrs. Serrano shuddered. "That's ridiculous," Mr. Murphy said.

"We have to be strong," Mr. Gorelick said. "If we cancel the parade, the prowler wins! We must go on with our lives."

"The parade will go on!" Mr. Jack said.

"Hooray for the parade!" Mr. Rogers said.

I knew I should tell the truth. I knew that if I didn't, things would probably get worse. But we had good reasons for spying. We were solving mysteries. We were trying to save Paz from a terrible curse.

If I said anything, I'd get in trouble. And so would Raymond.

And I'd promised him I wouldn't tell anyone about him. I'd promised.

Somehow, deep inside, I knew that was important.

CHAPTER 18
My Aura Gets Bluer

My T-shirt said CATONSVILLE NINE on the front and LEMON E. KICKIT on the back. It was gold and black, which clashed with the red-white-and-blue theme of the parade. But I didn't care. Roller derby was the most important thing.

Mr. Jack led the parade down Carroll Drive with the littler kids playing "Yankee Doodle" on kazoos. The Carters waved and cheered as Thea pulled Tessie and Bo in their wagon. Mr. Gorelick honked Old Donna's horn as the ancient car rolled slowly down the street, hung with flags and bunting. Lennie and Hugo had decorated their bikes and rode them proudly while their parents and Awa and Melina clapped. Troy and David hadn't bothered to decorate their bikes, but they rode them down the street anyway, terrorizing the spectators with their squirt guns.

Thea pulled her wagon over to Melina to say hello. "Don't Tessie and Bo look great?" She'd painted American flags on their faces.

Melina looked down her nose at them. "Yeah, they look great," she said without enthusiasm.

Strange. Why was Melina being so frosty to Thea?

"Pull!" Tessie ordered. "Pull us, Thea!"

Thea put her head down and pulled. She suddenly reminded me of Otis's horse, Esmeralda.

Paz wasn't there, and neither were Isabelle, Katie, or Lydia. I guess they were all too cool for the parade. I skated down the street alone. I couldn't do any fancy tricks without a partner, so I played the harmonica to make it less boring. I felt like an idiot — an idiot who had no friends. Everyone around me was either a little kid or an old person, and I was stuck in between.

"Hey there, Minty Fresh!" Mom and Dad waved to me from the sidelines. I pasted on a smile and waved back at them, but my heart wasn't in it.

The parade wrapped around the block and ended in front of the Gorelicks' house. Otis and Esmeralda waited for us, the cart loaded with watermelons and peaches and lemonade to sell. "Happy Fourth of July!" Otis called.

The barbecue ran through three backyards, from the Gorelicks' to our house to Wendy's. We lined up all the picnic tables we could find and fired up four grills.

I sat down on the front steps and took off my roller skates. I wondered what Raymond was doing right now. Otis sat on his cart drinking lemonade. Esmeralda munched on a watermelon that had smashed on the street.

"How's your aura doing?" Otis called.

I stood awkwardly in front of him while he studied the air around me. "What color is it now?" I asked.

He squinted. "Ooh, that aura has blued. You're a deep muddy blue now. How are you feeling?"

"Blue," I replied. "Lonely."

"Yep, I can see that."

"Can I do something to change it?" I asked.

"Your aura's just a reflection of how you feel inside," Otis said. "Change how you feel, and the aura will change color."

"But how can I change how I feel?" I didn't see what good it was knowing the color of my aura when I already knew how I felt — lousy.

"Hey, if I knew the answers to everything, I wouldn't be driving this cart selling fruit," Otis said.

"But you do know the answers to some things," I said.

He nodded. "Try me."

"What do you know about the Witch Lady?"

"Mm-hmmm." He drained his cup. "Not too much, I'll tell you that. I drive over that way once in a while, just to see how things are going. I used to see a little boy over there, a couple years ago. All by himself, playing outside in all kinds of weather, even the rain and the freezing cold. Once I asked him why he didn't go inside and get warm and he said he couldn't — the door was locked. And I said, 'Where's your mama?' and he said, 'She's inside sleeping.'"

He poured himself some more lemonade and a cup for me. "Then what happened?" I asked.

"Well, I didn't like seeing this boy outside in the cold and the wet, so I knocked on the door. The boy said, 'She won't answer,' and sure enough, not a peep came from the house. I knocked again, harder this time, but nothing happened. I tried the knob, but it was locked, just like the boy said. Short of breaking in through a window, I didn't see what else I could do. I walked around the house, peering inside, looking for that boy's mother, and finally I saw her lying on the kitchen floor, out cold."

This was a terrible and fascinating story. "Was she dead?"

"No, no, she just drank too much liquor or something like that, I suppose."

"And is she the Witch Lady?" I asked.

"The very same." He offered me a peach. I rubbed the fuzz and waited to hear more.

"Well, after that, I didn't see that boy around anymore for a long time. Early last spring, those construction fellas started clearing the fields and building those new houses, and a few weeks ago I saw the boy again. I asked him where he'd been, but he wouldn't tell me."

"He's got a secret," I said.

"Looks that way."

Up the street, Paz limped toward us. She didn't need crutches, but her ankle was tender. That reminded me . . .

"Otis, do you know anything about voodoo curses?"

"Ha! I know plenty. Too much. My high school girl-friend made a mean love potion. How do you think she got me to take her to the prom?"

"Someone put a curse on Paz," I said. "I'm trying to figure out who it is."

"That won't be easy," Otis said. "But if I were you, I'd look for a doll. Find the voodoo doll, you find the source of the curse."

"Thanks, Otis."

Paz finally made it to the cart. Otis gave her a cup of lemonade. "Cures what ails you."

"Even sprained ankles?" Paz asked.

"Sure, why not?"

Paz drank the lemonade. From the backyard I heard Mr. Jack yell, "Hamburgers ready! Who wants one?"

"That's what I've been waiting for." Otis jumped off his cart and jogged over to the picnic. I walked slowly across the grass with Paz.

"Sorry I didn't come to the parade," she said. "It gets tiring standing on one foot."

"That's okay."

"How was it?"

"Boring and stupid."

"I figured."

We settled at a picnic table. I got us each a hamburger, and we ate among our neighbors.

"Is this seat taken?" Wendy sat beside Paz, her paper plate loaded with a ketchupy burger and potato salad.

"Mind if I sit here?" Mr. Rogers sat down next to me. He had a hamburger patty, no bun, with pickles and no potato salad. And a Diet Rite cola.

Hmmm.

I glanced at Paz, but she didn't seem to notice. Then I remembered: Paz didn't know about the secret diet sabotage.

That was my other friend, Raymond.

"I don't know why I don't just give up," Mr. Rogers said to Wendy. "My diet's not working anyway." He laughed and patted his belly, but it was a sad laugh.

Wendy, who's tall and thin, nodded and smiled, her mouth full of burger, as if she understood. After she swallowed she said, "I think you look fine, Ken."

"Thanks, Wendy." Mr. Rogers looked down at his plate. "It's for health reasons, you know, the diet. I have to stay healthy to keep up with Troy there."

Troy and David were sitting at the end of the table, competing to see who could stuff the most potato salad into his mouth at one time. Mayonnaise dribbled down David's chin. Potatoes spewed out of Troy's overstuffed mouth.

"Any sign of Phoebe yet?" Mr. Rogers asked.

Wendy's eye grew wet. "No. I've posted signs everywhere. I check the animal shelter every day. Looks like she's just . . . gone."

Mr. Rogers's eyes welled up too. That surprised me. Again I checked to see if Paz was watching this, but she was studying Kip and Melina at the next table. Melina was talking to Kip, but his attention kept wandering away to the buffet line. She'd tap his hand, and he'd look at her and nod to show he was listening. But he obviously wasn't.

"Why don't you and I take a drive later and see if we can find her?" Mr. Rogers said to Wendy.

Fwat! A watermelon seed suddenly plastered itself to Mr. Rogers's face. He glared down the table at Troy, who held a straw to his mouth. *Fwat!* He shot another seed at Wendy.

Mr. Rogers jumped up. "Troy Rogers, you come with me." He rounded the table, grabbed Troy by the arm, and led him away. "When will you learn to behave? We're going to have a talk, Buster. . . ."

Troy didn't look scared. He was laughing. So was David. David shot some seeds at Troy as Mr. Rogers dragged him away.

Wendy sighed and ate her hamburger. DeeDee and Claudia sat down next to David. Wendy watched them while she ate.

"Where's Troy? Getting punished again?" Claudia asked.

"I don't know," David mumbled.

"You never know anything," DeeDee said.

David slumped in his seat. I think Wendy felt sorry for him, because she said, "Girls, that's no way to talk to your brother."

But they only laughed and walked away to get some ice cream.

"Don't listen to them, David," Wendy said. "They're just trying to psych you out."

"Who cares?" David said.

Paz tapped my hand to get my attention. "Minty, watch this."

From the buffet line, Thea waved to Kip and called, "Medium-rare?"

He called back, "Yeah!"

Melina turned around and glared at Thea.

"Did you see that look?" Paz asked.

"Yeah," I said. "Something's definitely wrong."

"I've never seen them so cold to each other before," Paz said.

Neither had I. The Fourth of July sure seemed to bring out the worst in people.

After dinner I took a walk in the woods. Otis and Esmeralda had left. Soon it would be dark. I stopped at the Secret Tree and reached inside.

I wanted to find an answer. To something. To anything.

But instead, I found another secret.

I'm betraying my best friend in a terrible way.

All the secrets were sad. But this one really hurt me. Because to me, best friends are sacred. And when this person's best friend found out about the betrayal, that friendship would be over.

I put the secret back in the hole. I wanted Crazy Ike to eat it. I wanted it to go away.

I walked home in the dusk. Mr. Jack was setting off some fireworks he'd bought in Virginia. He did this every year. He didn't have a permit, but a lot of the things Mr. Jack did were illegal. That's just the way he was.

Everyone in the neighborhood was gathered in my backyard, faces turned to the sky. The fireworks bathed them in colors, red, white, blue, green. . . .

They all have their secrets, I thought. *Each person's real life is a mystery.*

The fireworks exploded, commemorating a war for independence, while all around me people fought their private battles. Even the Mean Boys. Sister versus brother, friend versus friend, son versus father . . . they all had private battles that no one understood except for them.

I wanted to understand. But the more I spied, the more mystery I uncovered. I'd never know the whole story. There was so much I couldn't guess.

One of these people was betraying his or her best friend. Was Troy betraying David?

Was Melina betraying Thea?

My eyes fell on Paz. A thought fought its way to the front of my mind, a thought so awful I could hardly stand to think it. But it pushed its way through and made itself known.

Was Paz betraying me?

And then, one final possibility: Was Raymond?

CHAPTER 19
The Catnapper

On the fifth of July, I walked through the woods to visit Raymond. I couldn't resist a stop at the Secret Tree on the way.

The secret about betraying a best friend was gone, but there was a new secret — a juicy one — in its place.

I know where Wendy's cat is. And I'm not telling.

I put it in my pocket and ran the rest of the way through the woods to show Raymond.

"Look." I pulled the new secret out of my pocket. "The mystery deepens."

Raymond read the slip of paper. "Let's get the book." We studied the secret notebook, pondering the pictures of everyone in the neighborhood. Which of these people was betraying a friend? Which one was hiding a cat? It was impossible to tell.

Anyone was capable of anything. That's how it seemed to me now.

"Maybe we should lie low for a while," I said. "The whole neighborhood's on edge because of the 'prowler.'"

"But what about Wendy? You keep telling me how upset she is about her cat."

"That's true. She practically broke down in sobs last night at the barbecue."

"And what if someone is treating Phoebe bad?" Raymond said. "Or hurting her? We've got to rescue her!"

He was right. There was no time to lose. "My top suspects are the Mean Boys."

"They're your top suspects for every case," Raymond said.

"Because they do a lot of bad things," I said.

"We still haven't figured out who put a curse on Paz," Raymond added. "We've hardly solved any of these secret mysteries at all. We have a lot of work to do." He paused. "You haven't told anyone about me, have you?"

"No! No one," I swore, and it was true. Though I didn't mention the story Otis had told me the night before. He had never said the name of the boy who was locked out of his house.

"I believe you," Raymond said. "You're a good friend. But you have to keep your promise. You promised to keep my secret — remember?"

"I remember. Don't worry, Raymond. I'll keep your secret."

"Thanks. Now let's find out everyone else's secret!" He cackled with glee.

I know, it didn't make sense. And it wasn't fair. His secret was to be kept, and everyone else's were fair game. But isn't that how everybody feels?

It was an eerie night. Crickets chirped and cicadas whirred, night birds sang, music drifted through the darkness. The lawns were charcoal carpets in the moonlight. Woodlawn Road felt like a movie set — almost real, but not quite.

Somewhere off in the distance, a cat yowled.

"Maybe that's Phoebe," Raymond said.

"It's coming from that direction." I pointed toward Carroll Drive.

We glided like ghosts through yards, past houses sleeping and wakeful. The Carters' house was dark except for a flickering TV light in the living room. Thea was babysitting again.

"Let's stop and peek in on Thea," I whispered. I knew it was risky, but I couldn't resist.

We crept up to the living room window. Thea sat on the couch as a horror movie flickered on the screen, the sound down low.

But Thea wasn't watching the movie. And she wasn't alone.

A boy was on the couch with her. And they were kissing. A lot.

"Who's that?" I hissed.

"Shhh!" Raymond clapped his hand over my mouth.

I could only see the back of the boy's head. I tried to think of boys Thea liked. She hadn't mentioned anyone in particular. Who could this be?

Thea pulled away from the boy and laughed at something he said. The boy stood up and walked into the kitchen. Thea sat up and smoothed her hair.

I was shaking. Raymond clamped his arms around me, trying to keep me quiet.

The boy came back from the kitchen with two sodas. I could see his face now.

It was Kip.

CHAPTER 20
Thea's Secret

I must have gasped, I don't remember, but Thea jumped up as if she'd heard something. Raymond pushed me flat against the wall. I was breathing hard and fast.

"That's Kip Murphy!" I whispered. "That's the boy Melina likes!"

"Shhh!" Raymond pulled me along the wall of the house. We had to get away fast, before Thea caught us. We ran out of the yard, keeping to the shadows, and didn't stop until we were safely in the woods. Thea wouldn't follow us that far. She'd be too scared of getting attacked by the Man-Bat or the prowler.

Everybody knew Melina liked Kip. Thea knew it better than anyone.

But Thea liked Kip too.

I remembered the night Raymond and I saw Melina spying on Kip, when she ran away crying. Now I could guess why.

She must have seen Thea kissing Kip. That's why she was mad at Thea.

Melina was Thea's best friend. And Thea was betraying her.

Once I got over my shock, Raymond and I swept quietly through the neighborhood, looking for Phoebe. We saw Isabelle and Lydia swimming at night in Isabelle's pool with Isabelle's older brother, Martin. We saw Katie Park sitting in her family room with her father, watching TV. I wondered why she wasn't swimming with Isabelle — she sure didn't look like she was having fun at home.

We heard Mr. Serrano telling David — very loudly — that if he wasn't careful he'd end up loading fruit crates for the rest of his life. We heard Mr. Rogers singing a love song out of tune. We saw Wendy on her porch, whistling and calling, "Phoebe! Come back, girl!" We found two stray cats and were barked at by three dogs. But we didn't find Phoebe.

I kept my curtains open when I went to bed that night, so I could watch the moon. Clouds swept across it, casting shadows.

Nothing was going well.

Someone knew where Wendy's cat was — lonely, brokenhearted Wendy — and wouldn't tell. Thea and Kip were sneaking around behind Melina's back. Someone was sabotaging his father's diet, and someone else had put a curse on Paz.

Even Raymond had secrets he wouldn't share. Like why did he live in the model home?

A pit of loneliness opened up in my stomach. I reached for my harmonica.

CHAPTER 21
Lennie's Secret

The next day, I walked up to the Calderons' house. Before I had a chance to knock on their back door, I heard shrieking from the kitchen. Something told me not to interrupt — probably my newly sharpened spy sense. Instead of knocking, I ran down the back stairs and hid behind the trash cans.

"Why can't I go?" Lennie shouted.

"You're not invited," Paz said.

Invited where? I wondered.

"You can't keep me out. I belong to the pool too, you know!"

I also belonged to the pool.

"So go. But don't come near me and my friends. Stay in the baby pool with Hugo and Robbie."

Awa barked out something in Chinese, effectively stopping the fight. Paz burst out the kitchen door and limped down the back stairs, her ankle still wrapped in gauze, a towel flung over her shoulder. She hopped onto her bike and rode away. She never noticed me cowering behind the trash cans. Off to the pool, no doubt. To be with her friends. Who didn't include me.

Awa yelled some more at Lennie, who said, "All right, all right," and stomped away.

I stayed hidden, listening. But all I heard now was the radio switch on and Awa bustling around the kitchen, humming along.

Just behind me, down low near the ground, a light flickered on in the basement window.

I couldn't resist taking a peek.

Lennie was alone in the basement. She flung herself on the couch and picked up her book, *Man-Bat! The Story of Man-Bat*. She pulled out another, smaller book hidden inside the Man-Bat tell-all. She opened the second book and read a passage very intently. I tried to make out the title. I thought I saw a picture of a woman in a turban on the cover, and the words *Voodoo, Hoodoo, and You*.

Lennie put down the book and opened a cupboard. She moved aside some games and toys and pulled out a wooden box that looked like it might hold chess pieces.

She opened the box and pulled out a red cloth doll. It had a long, black braid down its back, four tiny barrettes in its hair, and Paz's wallet-size school picture glued to its face. The doll was stuck full of pins.

A voodoo doll. A Paz voodoo doll.

Lennie glanced at the voodoo book again, then muttered something and picked up a pin. She pushed into the doll's forehead.

"So it's you!" I gasped. I couldn't help it. I was so shocked the words flew out of my mouth before I could stop them.

Lennie looked up and saw me crouched outside the window. "Hey! What are you doing there?"

She dropped the doll and ran up the stairs. She was coming for me.

My legs tensed, ready to run. But Lennie had seen me. She'd find me one way or another. There was no place to hide in this neighborhood.

The kitchen door slammed open, and Lennie appeared at the top of the stairs. She glared down at me where I huddled by the trash cans. My knees shook as I straightened my legs to face her. She was only nine, but anyone mean enough to put a curse on her own sister was someone to be scared of.

She walked slowly down the back stairs and stood face-to-face with me. "Let's talk about what you *think* you saw," she said.

"You put a curse on your own sister."

"She deserves it." Lennie's gaze was clear and hard as glass.

"But why? What did Paz do to you?"

"You know what she did." The glassy stare cracked and she looked away. "She lost Marcella."

Marcella. Lennie's toy cat. Which Paz borrowed last Halloween to complete her cute witch costume. The Witch Lady had snatched Marcella away.

"Marcella was my favorite toy," Lennie said. "I slept with her since I was a baby! The Witch Lady probably has her locked up somewhere, rotting in that horrible, scary house! And Paz doesn't care." She flounced around in a lame imitation of carefree Paz. "'Oh, well, so I lost your favorite toy. Get over it!'"

"Paz cares," I said. "But what can she do about it?"

"If she cared, she'd get Marcella back." Lennie crossed her arms and jutted out her jaw.

"She can't get Marcella back," I said. "She didn't mean to lose her. You have to stop voodooing Paz and forgive her. You're hurting her."

"She hurt me first. I'm not going to stop until I get Marcella back."

"Then I'm going to tell Paz you put a curse on her," I said.

"You can't do that." Lennie's jutting jaw quivered. "She'll kill me!"

"She deserves to know," I said. "And as her best friend, it's my duty to tell her."

"Best friend," Lennie spat. "Is she as good a friend as she is a sister?"

I couldn't answer that. I didn't know firsthand what kind of sister Paz was.

"She's Pax A. Punch," I said. "And I'm Minty Fresh. That's all that matters."

"Go ahead and tell her. I don't care," Lennie said. "I'm not removing the curse until I get Marcella back."

This was bad news. How much more cursing could Paz take?

"Maybe if you apologize, she'll forgive you for cursing her," I said.

"Fat chance," Lennie said.

"We'll see."

I went home and got my bike for the ride to the pool. I had something important to tell Paz. Something that could really help her. And then she'd remember what a good friend I was.

Chapter 22
A Warning

At the pool, Paz lay on a towel near the deep end, lined up beside Isabelle, Katie, and Lydia. Her ankle wrap was gone. I guess it would have made a funny tan line. The girls all wore bikinis, their skin gleaming, their eyes closed against the sun. And each girl wore a row of four silver barrettes in her hair.

I cast a shadow over Paz. She blinked and shaded her eyes.

"Minty? You're blocking my sun."

"Do you have a headache?" I stared at her forehead.

"What?"

"Any pain in your head at all?" Lennie had stuck a pin in the voodoo doll's forehead. What if that gave Paz a brain tumor? The symptoms might not show up for years.

Paz closed her eyes again. "My head feels fine, Minty. Can you step out of my sun, please?"

"Paz, I've got something important to tell you." I sat down beside her on the hot concrete, on the far side of Isabelle, careful not to shade her.

"So tell me."

I glanced at Isabelle and her friends. Katie and Lydia had opened their eyes and lifted their heads just enough so they could see what was going on.

"It's private," I said in a low voice.

"You might as well tell her in front of us." Isabelle spoke without opening her eyes. "There are no secrets between friends. Whatever it is, Paz will tell us anyway — won't you, Paz?"

"Definitely," Paz said. "Go ahead, Minty."

I didn't think this was a good idea, but she asked for it. . . .

"Someone has put a curse on you," I said. "A voodoo curse. For real."

Lydia and Katie giggled.

Paz propped herself up on her elbows. "What are you talking about? I'm not cursed."

"Oh, no?" I said. "That mysterious stomachache you had a few weeks ago, that unexplained rash, the itchy nose, your twisted ankle —?"

"I've had a lot of bad luck lately," Paz said.

"It's no accident," I insisted. "Someone's trying to hurt you on purpose — and I know who."

The other girls laughed, and Paz laughed with them. "Who? The Witch Lady?"

That really sent the other girls into hysterics. "The Witch Lady!" Isabelle cried. "You don't really believe she's a witch, do you?"

"Paz, I'm serious," I said. "At first I thought it might be the Witch Lady, but it turns out —"

"I know — a zombie!" Lydia said.

"The Man-Bat!" Paz added. "Minty, you're worse than Lennie."

They all cracked up. I felt like I'd barged in on a secret club where everyone knew the code except for me.

I tried to remember the last time Paz felt like my friend — my *best* friend. Was it at her birthday party in May? Or at our elementary school graduation, when we wore matching daisies in our hair and promised to be best friends forever?

Whenever it was, it seemed like a long time ago.

I gave her one more chance. "You don't believe me?"

Paz rolled over on her stomach, resting her head on her arms. "Come on, Minty. You have to admit it sounds ridiculous."

"All right. Fine. I won't tell you." I stood up, blocking her sun again. "I'm going to get a snowball. Want to come with me?" Maybe if I got her alone, she'd stop being silly and listen.

"No," she said, her voice muffled by her towel. "Why don't you get me a blood orange snowball? Just make sure it's not poisoned. Or cursed, or whatever." The girls laughed again.

"Okay."

The lifeguard blew his whistle for Adult Swim. Kids

climbed out of the pool and raced to the snack bar. By the time I got there, the line snaked all the way back to the women's changing room. I waited, fuming. Why was I even getting Paz a snowball when she was being so horrible to me?

David, Connie, and DeeDee were in line in front of me. "What did you learn in summer school this morning?" DeeDee asked David.

"Nothing," David said.

"Oh, come on," Connie said. "You must have worked on something."

"Grammar and spelling," David said.

"Spelling?" Connie said. "Here, I'll test you. How do you spell *knapsack*?"

David thought for a second. Then he said, "Easy. N-"

"*Bzzzzt!* Wrong." Connie and DeeDee laughed. "It's K-N-A-"

The back of David's neck turned red, and it wasn't from the sun. "Who cares anyway?" he said.

"Not you, I guess," Connie said. "You're zombie diet food."

"What's that mean?" David asked.

"Slim pickings for brains," Connie replied. "Zombie diet food, zombie diet food," she and DeeDee chanted.

"Shut up," David said.

Im so stoopid, I thought. *Im affraid something is rong with my brane.*

And suddenly, David wasn't a Mean Boy. He was just a boy.

They reached the front of the line and bought candy. I was starting to feel sorry for David. His sisters made Thea look like a fairy godmother.

When it was my turn, I ordered two snowballs. I carried them back through the breezeway and along the side of the pool to the deep end, where Paz and the other girls had been sitting.

They were gone.

I scanned the pool grounds, but there was no sign of them. I went outside to check for Paz's bike. It wasn't there. Far up the hill, four girls rode away on their bikes, chrome fenders flashing in the sun.

Paz had run away from me. From me, her best friend.

Now it was my turn to feel stupid.

I sat down and slurped my spearmint snowball. Then I drank the melty remains of Paz's.

I wasn't going to go chasing after her.

CHAPTER 23
Slayer's Secret

I rode my bike home the long way, up Carroll Drive, because that was the way to Isabelle's house, and I guess I was half hoping I'd catch up to them somehow and they'd say, *There you are! We were looking for you! Come hang out with us!*

That was one voice whispering to me. Another said, *I'm betraying my best friend in a terrible way.*

It sounded a lot like Paz, just then.

I was learning this thing about secrets: Even if they're not about you, once you know them, they feel like they *could* be about you. Every secret connects to something inside of you, whether you know it at first or not.

As I cruised past Troy's house, I saw Slayer trotting across the yard, a mouse clenched between his teeth. He ran to a basement window at the side of the house and meowed. He scratched on the window, trying to get in. He meowed again, that wild, spooky mewl cats sometimes do, which makes them sound possessed by demons.

Silly Slayer, I thought. I parked my bike on the grass and went over to see what he was up to. He pressed his head against the glass in frustration. I bent down to pet him, but he ignored me. I tried to peel the window open for him, but of course it was locked.

Then I saw what he was meowing at. Perched on top of the basement couch, waving her poofy white tail like crazy and kneading the scratchy plaid fabric with her paws, was Phoebe.

I ran around to the front of the house and rang the doorbell. No one answered, and nothing stirred in the house. Then I remembered: Mr. Rogers was probably at work, and Troy was doing time at Thea's day camp.

I heard a speedy *pfft pfft pfft* and the skid of rubber on asphalt. "Whatcha doing, loser?" Troy yelled. He dropped his bike in the driveway and walked up to where I stood on his front porch. "Selling Girl Scout cookies? Hmmm, I don't see any boxes. . . ."

"You have Wendy's cat," I spat at him. He stiffened.

Aha! I'd caught him.

"What are you talking about?" he said.

"You catnapper!" I cried. "What are you going to do with her?"

"Shh! Shh!" Troy took a key from his pocket and quickly opened the front door. "Get inside before anybody hears you." Slayer slipped inside just as Troy was closing the door.

"Phoebe!" I ran to the basement stairs and opened the door. "Phoebe, I'm here to save you! You can come out now!"

Phoebe meowed at the foot of the stairs but didn't come up. Slayer ran down, the mouse still dangling from his jaws.

"Why did you do it, Troy?" I demanded.

Troy raised his arms in surrender. "I didn't catnap anybody. She sneaked in through the basement window and wouldn't leave. She and Slayer are in love. They're living together down there."

"Really?" At the foot of the stairs, Slayer had dropped the mouse at Phoebe's feet and was licking her behind the ears. "But why didn't you tell Wendy? She's going crazy looking for her."

Troy dropped his arms. "None of your business, okay? Take the cat to Wendy if you want. She's only going to run back here, though."

"I think you should take Phoebe back and tell Wendy you're sorry for hiding her," I said. "Come on, Troy. Tell me why you did it." I sat at the kitchen island to show him I wasn't going anywhere until I got an answer. He stood by the fridge, picking at a kitchen magnet and not saying anything. Next to the fridge was a jar of diet shake mix.

"Hey —" I began. "You're dad's on a diet, isn't he?"

"Yeah. So?"

I tried to think of a way to bring up this sensitive topic without revealing that I knew Troy's secrets. "So how come he hasn't lost any weight?"

Troy shrugged, but he wouldn't look at me. *Guilty*, I thought.

"He's just built chubby, I guess. He says no woman will look at him until he loses thirty pounds."

Sabotage, I thought. *That's exactly what Troy wants.* But back to the more important issue — Wendy's cat. "Why didn't your Dad return Phoebe to Wendy?"

"He doesn't know Phoebe's here," Troy confessed. "The basement is my territory. Believe me, when he finds out, he's going to be mad. He really likes *Wendy*." He made a face.

"Don't you like her? She's nice!" I said.

"I just . . . I don't want my dad to like her. Or her to like my dad," Troy said. "Slayer had to go and fall in love with her dumb cat, and I was afraid that would give Dad ideas."

"Ideas?"

"Yeah. Like, he would think if Slayer and Phoebe are a couple, maybe he and Wendy should be a couple too. So we could all be one big happy family."

"What's wrong with that? Wendy's nice, and your dad is lonely —"

"He is not! Anyway, how would you know?"

"I can just tell." I wasn't about to say I knew because I spied on him singing love songs with the radio in the kitchen.

"He can't have a girlfriend," Troy said. "If he gets a girlfriend, that means . . . that means . . ."

"What?"

Troy kicked the bottom of the refrigerator so hard he made a dent.

"That means my mom isn't coming back."

"Maybe not," I said. "But even if your dad never gets a girlfriend, that doesn't mean your mom will come back."

Me and my big mouth.

Troy's face puckered like he'd just sucked on a lemon. It struck me that he'd looked sour all year. I thought it was a Mean Boy face. But now I realized it was a hurt face.

"You don't know anything." Troy ran out of the house. He picked up his bike and slammed it down on the driveway. Then he picked it up again and sped away.

"*Meow . . . Purr . . .*" Downstairs, the two cats were happily grooming each other. It was a shame to separate them. But Wendy would find a way to let them be together, I was sure.

I walked down the steps and reached for Phoebe. Slayer hissed at me. I jerked my hand back. He hissed again.

Troy should be the one to return Phoebe, I thought. It was his secret. He was the one who had to clear it up.

I heard his bike skid into the driveway. He'd only gone around the block. He kicked open the screen door. "You still here? This is my house, you know."

"If you don't take Phoebe home, I'm going to tell on you," I said.

"You would, tattletale," Troy scowled. He went downstairs and scooped Phoebe up. "Sorry, dude." Slayer didn't dare hiss at him.

I wasn't really going to tell on him. I just knew that he'd never do it unless I made him do it. Maybe returning Phoebe would help him get free of his secret. When he saw the look on Wendy's face, he might feel good about her and glad he could make someone happy.

"Don't worry, Slayer — you can visit whenever you want," I said. Slayer's eyes shrank to angry slits.

Troy started for the kitchen door with Phoebe in his arms. Mr. Rogers's car pulled into the driveway, nearly running over Troy's bike.

Troy hesitated. "What do I do now?"

"It's okay," I said. "Maybe he'll go with you."

Mr. Rogers walked into the kitchen, carrying a bag of groceries. He stopped and stared at the fluffy white cat in Troy's arms.

"Troy! You found Phoebe!" He hugged Troy and Phoebe, then gave a little jump. "Where was she? Hi, Minty!"

When I saw how happy he was that Phoebe was safe, I knew I was right. He liked Wendy for sure.

"She was hiding down in the basement with Slayer all this time," Troy admitted.

"They're in love," I added.

"You don't say." Mr. Rogers fluffed Phoebe's fur.

"Good for you, Slayer! Come on — let's go tell Wendy! She'll flip!"

He burst out the door. I thought he was going to dance across his backyard on the way to Wendy's house. Troy held Phoebe like he was carrying a corpse to a funeral. I trotted along beside him.

"It's going to be great," I whispered to Troy. "You'll see."

Mr. Rogers whistled as he jogged up the four steps to Wendy's front door and rang the bell. "Oh, Wendy, I've got some news for you. . . ." he sang.

Wendy opened the door. Phoebe leaped out of Troy's arms and ran to her. She screamed a happy scream. She hugged Phoebe. "Oh, Ken," she said to Mr. Rogers. "I'm so happy, I could kiss you!"

She kissed Mr. Rogers on the cheek. Then she kissed Troy, who made an extra-sour face. She even kissed me.

The rest is neighborhood history.

CHAPTER 24
Spying Runs in the Family

I was so happy about Phoebe and Wendy and Mr. Rogers that I almost forgot how sad I was about Paz running away from me.

"Mom!" I ran into the kitchen. "Phoebe's back!"

Mom wasn't in the kitchen. I spread a glob of peanut butter on some bread and ate it as I walked down the hall toward Mom and Dad's room. "Mom? I've got some Wendy gossip for you!"

Mom came out of Thea's room and shut the door. She had an odd look on her face. Kind of a guilty twitch.

"Is Thea home?" I asked.

"She's still at work." The twitch deepened.

"So what were you doing in her . . . Oh." I understood. Mom was snooping in Thea's room.

"Don't you want a plate for your sandwich?" Mom led me back to the kitchen. As if it was so easy to change the subject. She took a plate out of the cupboard and slid it under my half-eaten sandwich.

"Did you find anything?" I asked.

"What do you mean?"

"In Thea's room."

"No." She poured herself a glass of iced tea and sat down at the kitchen table. "I'm sorry, honey. I know it looks bad. It's just that I'm so worried about Thea, always sneaking out. I never know what she's up to. I want her to be safe."

I knew what Thea was up to — at least I thought I did. Kissing Kip Murphy while her best friend seethed. Mom would probably like to know that. But if I told Thea's secret, wouldn't that betray her?

"Don't worry, I get it." I couldn't judge Mom for spying on Thea since I'd spent most of the summer so far spying on people. "I won't tell Thea."

"Thanks, Minty. I feel terrible. But I don't know what else to do."

I knew what she meant. Once you start spying, it's hard to stop. The more you find out, the more you need to know.

My brain was getting all muddled.

"What's the gossip?" Mom asked.

"We found Phoebe," I reported. "She was hiding in the Rogerses' basement. She and Slayer fell in love, which will work out great because I think Wendy and Mr. Rogers will probably be living together soon."

"Really?" Mom's face lit up. "That's wonderful! I'm so happy for Wendy. She's been lonely for so long."

"So has Mr. Rogers," I said.

"So he has," Mom said. "See? Everything works out in the end."

"But it's not the end yet," I said. "Some other bad thing could happen to them later."

"Well — yes. You're right, Minty. But for now, they're happy."

"For now."

"That's all we can ask for, right?"

I guessed it was.

I spent the rest of the afternoon lying in the hammock out back, practicing sad songs on my harmonica. That terrible moment of finding Paz gone kept replaying in my head. Its meaning had really sunk in deep.

Thea came home from work just before dinner. I heard her shut herself in her room and turn on some music. I went upstairs and knocked on her door.

"Come in."

She was lying on her bed. "Hey, Minty." She smiled at me. She seemed calm for once. "Feels like I haven't seen you all summer."

"That's because you've been busy," I said.

"You're right. I have been busy, between babysitting and the day camp and . . . other stuff."

I didn't ask what the other stuff was, because I knew.

"Guess what? Mr. and Mrs. Carter are going to have another baby," Thea said. "But don't tell Mom. They haven't told anyone yet."

"Then how do you know? Did Mrs. Carter tell you?"

"Not exactly . . ." She looked away. "I found some special pregnancy vitamins in her medicine chest. And a really sweet card from Mr. Carter."

When I'm babysitting, after the kids are asleep, I snoop through the parents' drawers and closets, I thought.

"What did it say?" I asked.

"It had a picture of a rose on the front, and it said he loves her and he's so excited about the new baby. I just happened to see it in Mrs. Carter's, um . . ." She couldn't quite look at me.

"Mrs. Carter's what?"

"Underwear drawer."

"Underwear drawer!" I could definitely cross that secret off the Unsolved list.

"Tessie's forehead felt hot, and I was looking for the thermometer," Thea said.

"Sure you were. Everyone keeps thermometers in their underwear drawer."

Thea tossed a pillow at me. "Don't tell anyone, okay?"

"I won't."

I tossed the pillow back on the bed. I picked up a book from her night table and paged through it without really seeing it. Then I put down the book and picked up a sea-shell. I wanted to ask her advice about something, but I was nervous.

"Minty, would you cut it out?" Thea said. Then she looked at me — really looked at me — and asked, "Hey, are you all right?"

I put down the seashell and sat beside her on the bed.

"Come on, tell me what's the matter." She patted her extra pillow. I stretched out beside her. I must have looked sad, because she didn't even yell at me about touching her stuff.

"I'm afraid that Paz doesn't like me anymore," I confessed.

"Why do you think that?"

"Today at the pool, she was with Isabelle and those other girls, and they made fun of me," I explained. The memory of that moment choked up in my chest. "I went to the snack bar to get us some snowballs and . . . Paz . . . and . . . and the other girls . . ." I was on the verge of tears, struggling to get the words out. "They left with-out me. Paz just left me there. They ran away from me. Without saying good-bye or anything."

"Oh." Thea wrapped her arm around me. "Poor Minty. That's a terrible feeling."

I started to cry, just a little. I pressed my face against Thea's shoulder. My big sister.

"Sixth grade starts in a month," I burbled. "And I won't have any friends. Paz will be off with the seventh graders, and they don't want me around."

Thea hugged me. "That's ridiculous. Paz is still your friend! She's just going through a phase, like trying on different personalities. A lot of people do that in middle school, you'll see. You'll probably do it too. Like one day you'll be Minty Fresh, tough roller derby girl. And the next day you'll paint your fingernails purple and see how it feels to be glam and girly. And then maybe you'll start wearing black turtlenecks and reading poetry."

"I don't think I'm going to go through those phases," I said. "I know who I am. I feel like I'm always going to be just the same."

"You'll always be you," Thea said. "But that doesn't mean you won't change."

"But what if I change in one direction and Paz changes in another, and we move so far apart we can't ever be friends again?"

Thea frowned thoughtfully and gave me a squeeze. "I don't think that's going to happen. You and Paz have a soul connection. But listen — there's one big lesson I learned in middle school. You can't force someone to be your friend. You can be nice and fun and try your hardest to make people like you, but either they will or they won't. And if one person doesn't like you, that's okay. Someone else will. You'll always have friends, Minty. You're very likable."

I lifted my head. Did Thea just call me likable? "I thought you thought I was a pest."

"I do. But you're a likable pest."

I hoped she was right. I felt like a very *un*likable pest.

"Why don't you go over there and talk to her now? Maybe she only ran away because Isabelle told her to."

"But that's not very friendly."

"No, but sometimes people are weak, and they do dumb things. Go talk to her, Mint."

Honestly, I didn't know why I was taking friendship advice from Thea. She had betrayed her best friend. But I had nowhere else to turn.

I could still help Paz. I could tell her who was cursing her, and why. She wouldn't listen to me at the pool. But maybe she'd listen to me now.

CHAPTER 25
My Secret

Awa was in the kitchen shucking corn for dinner. "Paz is upstairs," she told me.

I wondered where Lennie was. Maybe she was hiding from Paz, fearing her wrath. Little did she know I hadn't told on her — yet.

Paz was lying on her bed, reading. She looked up when I stopped in her doorway.

"Oh. Hey."

"Hi, Paz." I sat down on Lennie's bed. "I never got to finish what I was telling you at the pool."

"Oh, right. The curse!" Paz put down her book and sat up. She seemed warmer now that Isabelle wasn't around. Maybe Thea was right — it was Isabelle's influence that made Paz do mean things to me.

"It's Lennie," I told her. "She has a voodoo doll that looks like you. She's sticking pins in it and chanting spells or something, and that's what's causing all your problems."

"Lennie? Are you kidding me?"

"She admitted it. She hasn't forgiven you for losing Marcella."

Paz rolled her eyes. "That was months ago! And how does Lennie know how to do voodoo anyway?"

"She has an instruction book," I said.

"I don't believe it," Paz said. "She doesn't have that kind of power. It's got to be a coincidence."

"Maybe it is," I said. "But do you want to take that chance?"

"I do have a tiny headache." Paz rubbed her forehead. "How can I stop her?"

"She says she won't stop until she gets Marcella back."

"But the Witch Lady has her!" Paz complained. "What am I supposed to do, break into the Witch House?" She shuddered. "After what happened on Halloween, I'll never go back there again."

"Maybe you could buy her a new toy cat and tell her you're really, really sorry," I suggested. "I think she's mostly mad that you didn't apologize."

"I apologized," Paz said. "Nothing's ever enough for her. Maybe you can think of a way to get Marcella back. You're good at this stuff, Minty. What's the plan?"

"Try apologizing again."

"That won't work. Lennie's merciless. I *am* sorry about it. I just don't feel like saying it to her face. You know how it is with sisters."

"Yeah. I know."

"How did you find out about this, anyway?" Paz asked.

I swallowed. This was the part I felt kind of bad about. The part where I was spying on the Calderons. "Um, you know, I came over, and I just happened to see Lennie with the voodoo doll. . . ."

If she was suspicious, she didn't show it. "Thanks for telling me, Minty. I owe you."

"You don't owe me anything. But . . . will you tell me something?"

"Sure," Paz said.

"Why did you run away from me at the pool?"

Paz picked at her pink nail polish. "That was just a joke. It didn't mean anything. Isabelle thought it would be funny."

"Oh." I slid to the floor and leaned against Lennie's bed.

"I guess it wasn't that funny."

"Not really."

"It's just that — I wish you'd act more grown up sometimes, that's all."

"I act grown up," I insisted, though I didn't feel grown up at all.

"All that talk about voodoo and curses —"

"But it's true! You're the one who's cursed! I'm only trying to help you —"

"I know, it's just . . . in front of Isabelle and those guys . . ."

From where I was sitting, I could see the bottom shelf of Paz's night table. A fancy pink card lay on top of a pile of books.

I picked up the card. It said:

Pool Party! At Isabelle Barton's house.
Saturday, August 7, 3 PM. RSVP —

Paz yanked the card away from me. "Hey! That's private."

I was so shocked I could hardly speak. "Isabelle's having a party?"

"It's not a big party — just a few people. I'm sure she wanted to invite you. Her parents said she could only have a few friends —"

"Are you going?"

"Well . . . I haven't told her yet, one way or the other —"

"But are you planning to go?" I spied a new bikini hanging from her closet door. I had my answer. "You should go." I stood up to leave with tears in my eyes. "I know you'd rather go to her pool party than hang around doing nothing with me. It's okay. See you around."

"Minty, wait —"

I ran out of the house. She called to me out the window but I didn't stop, didn't look back. I ran home and grabbed a piece of paper and a pencil. I took them with me into the woods and walked to the Secret Tree.

I sat down and leaned against its wide, heavy trunk, and wrote down my secret.

I don't want to grow up. Ever.

I fed the secret into the hole. "There you go, Crazy Ike. Please eat this secret and make the pain go away."

The breeze kicked up, thrashing the treetops. My secret was out there now, on the wind.

CHAPTER 26
Surprise Lunch

I didn't see or speak to Paz for a couple of days. Feeling lonely, I walked through the woods to see Raymond. I had lots of news to tell him. Phoebe had been found. Mr. Rogers and Wendy definitely liked each other. Troy was the one who sabotaged his dad's diet. And Paz was going to parties without me.

On the way, I stopped by the Secret Tree and reached into the hole.

"What have you got for me today, Crazy Ike?" I asked.

I pulled out a secret. It said:

I made a special surprise lunch for my friend.

Ha! A happy secret for once. *Wait till Raymond sees this*, I thought.

I rang the doorbell of the model home. Raymond answered wearing a flowered apron over his jeans.

"I've got lots of news!" I said.

"Hooray!" Raymond let me in and shut the door behind me. "You can tell me over lunch."

He led me into the living room. The coffee table had been shoved aside and a sheet had been laid on the floor. The sheet was set for a picnic lunch, with a plate of bologna and American cheese slices, a loaf of white bread, a bottle of ketchup, a bowl of potato chips, two cans of grape soda, and a tall glass filled with wildflowers.

"Surprise!" he said. "I made us lunch!"

"Wow! Thanks, Raymond." I showed him the secret I'd just found. "So this is yours!"

He blushed. "Sit down at your place." I sat down on the floor while Raymond passed me the bread.

"But how did you know I was coming over today?" I asked.

"I didn't. But I knew you'd come sometime. So I made lunch for both of us every day."

"Oh." I guess I should have been happy to know that he'd looked forward to my visits so much, but instead I felt sad. I wondered what he did all day in this strange house by himself.

"Tell me the news!" Raymond piled his sandwich with bologna and cheese.

"Well, I found Phoebe." I took three slices of cheese for my sandwich. "She was in Troy's basement! He's the one who knew where she was all along and wouldn't tell."

Raymond nodded, his mouth full. He reached for

the secret notebook and began to update it, pasting Troy's secret under his picture.

"Also, Troy's the diet sabotager," I told him.

"Why was Troy doing all these weird things?" Raymond asked.

"Because his mother went away and he misses her," I explained. "He's afraid she won't come back if his dad gets a new girlfriend. But it's too late, because Mr. Rogers already likes Wendy. A lot."

"Does Troy like Wendy?" Raymond asked.

"No," I said. "Not very much."

"Hmm." He passed me the ketchup.

I made a face. "Ketchup on a cheese sandwich?"

"Try it. It's good."

I opened the bottle and squeezed. It spit out a few drops on a whoosh of air. I tried again. *Spfft*. Nothing.

"It's empty," I said.

"I'll do it." Raymond took the bottle from me and shook it, chanting, *"Shake and shake the ketchup bottle — none'll come and then a lot'll."*

Splurt. It worked! A stream of ketchup twirled onto my sandwich.

"My turn." I repeated the chant as I squirted ketchup on his sandwich. We topped them off with bread, then clinked our grape soda cans in a toast.

"Good lunch," I said.

"Thanks. I made it myself."

"When school starts, we can eat lunch together every day," I said. "Oh — except I'm starting middle school this year. What grade will you be in?"

"Sixth," he said.

"So we'll be in the same school," I said. "That's great!" So I *would* have a friend, even if Paz and I never made up.

"Well, maybe . . ." He concentrated on spreading his ketchup around on his bread. "I'm not sure what school I'm going to."

"When will you find out?" I asked.

He shrugged and picked up his harmonica. He started playing "You Are My Sunshine," which I always thought was a kind of sad song — the idea that someone would take your sunshine away.

"I've been practicing — look." I pulled my harmonica from my pocket and played along with him. We sounded very good together. I thought of those scenes in old movies where prisoners play the harmonica in jail as a way to pass the time.

After our harmonica break, Raymond fixed himself another sandwich. "What other news have you got?" he asked.

One of the secrets in the book caught my eye: *I'm betraying my best friend in a terrible way.* I couldn't help thinking of Paz.

"Isabelle Barton is having a pool party," I reported. "Paz is invited. But I'm not."

"Yes you are," Raymond said.

"No I'm not," I repeated. "I saw the invitation in Paz's room. I didn't get one."

"Well, you're invited to a better party," Raymond said. "A spy-on-Isabelle's-pool-party party."

"Yes . . ." An interesting idea. "We'll spy on the pool party! Who knows what we'll find out."

"Exactly. When is it?"

"This Saturday afternoon."

"Looks like we've got a new spy mission to plan." Raymond picked up his harmonica. "But first, another song."

We played our harmonicas the rest of the afternoon, until the bell rang and it was time for me to go home.

CHAPTER 27

The Prowler Strikes Again

Dad was off on Saturday. He settled into a hammock in the backyard with a glass of iced tea and a book. Mom, Thea, and I brought lunch to the patio so we could eat outside.

Mr. Gorelick stood in his backyard, hose in hand, watering his flower garden, while Mrs. Gorelick lounged in the sun. She rubbed tanning oil on her legs but kept her face carefully shaded with a straw hat and her cat's-eye sunglasses. Kelly, their dog, sat beside her with a blue ribbon in her hair, panting. All Kelly ever did was pant, pretty much, and yap once in a while.

"Ah," Dad said. "Isn't it a beautiful summer day? I'm not leaving this hammock until the mosquitoes come and get me."

"They'll eat you alive until you're nothing but a skeleton — right, Dad?" I brought his turkey sandwich over to him so he could eat it in the hammock.

"Now that's what I call service," Mr. Gorelick said.

"Would you like some iced tea?" Mom called from the patio.

"Thank you, Laurie. I love your iced tea."

"No sugar in mine," Mrs. Gorelick barked from under her hat.

Mom poured two glasses of iced tea and handed them to me to take to the Gorelicks.

Mr. Gorelick thanked me and wiped his forehead. "Looks like the prowler has struck again. Someone stole a harmonica out of our garage!"

I stiffened. *Did he say a harmonica?*

"A harmonica, of all things," Mr. Gorelick repeated. "With my two-hundred-dollar power drill right there for the taking."

"Right there." Mrs. Gorelick nodded and stroked Kelly.

"Not to mention Old Donna, who's priceless," Mr. Gorelick said. "I wonder if it happened during the Fourth of July picnic. I had the garage door open, and people were milling around all night."

Mom shook her head. "That's very strange. Why would someone steal a harmonica?"

"What do you mean?" Mr. Gorelick said. "It's just about the best instrument ever invented, after the organ. Especially if you've got someone to play rounds with. But Judy doesn't want to learn."

Mrs. Gorelick sighed. "There's too much spit involved."

"You'll never have any fun if you're afraid of a little spit," Mr. Gorelick said. "Hey, girls — you want me to set up the sprinkler for you after lunch? I've got to water the lawn anyway."

"Thanks, but I'm going to a pool party," Thea said.

"What? You are?" I cried.

"Sure," Thea said. "At Martin Barton's house."

So Thea was going to Isabelle's pool party too! Everyone had been invited except me. "Minty?" Mr. Gorelick prompted. "You know I hate to waste a sprinkler on plain old grass when kids could be enjoying it too."

"Not today," I said. "I've got things to do too."

"What kind of things?" Mom asked.

"Oh, you know." I tried to sound casual. "Just hanging around the neighborhood." Just hanging around, spying on the neighbors.

I'd scoped out Isabelle's house the day before, looking for good surveillance hideouts. The family who lived behind her, the Schwartzes, had a tree house. It overlooked Isabelle's backyard and pool but was well shaded by branches, so Isabelle wouldn't see me easily. Best of all, the Schwartzes were away on vacation.

"It's that kind of day." Dad swung gently in the hammock. He'd be asleep in half an hour, I could tell.

"Don't go too far," Mom warned.

"I won't." I knew the rule: Stay within the sound of the bell. And I would. I just might not come home if I heard it.

After lunch I stuffed my backpack with supplies for the mission — binoculars, a notebook and pen, water, juice, snacks, enough for both me and Raymond. He never had any good snacks, just that horrible bologna.

I picked up my harmonica from my night table and tooted a tune. Then I put it away in a drawer.

I should return the harmonica to Mr. Gorelick, I thought. *Raymond must have stolen it.*

But I didn't know that for sure. I didn't have proof.

And if I returned it, Raymond would get in trouble.

I felt sad. Raymond had given me a gift. A gift that I loved. But it wasn't much of a gift if it was stolen.

I shouldered my pack and set off to meet my partner in crime.

Chapter 28
The Pool Party

We sneaked into the Schwartzes' backyard and climbed up into the tree house. "This is the perfect hideout," Raymond said. "Good recon work, Minty."

It was a very comfortable tree house, with cushions to sit on and a low table to eat at. One window looked right down at Isabelle's pool and was close enough to hear a lot of conversation too. I pulled my binoculars out of my backpack. "In case we need to zoom in for detail."

"I brought some too." Raymond pulled a small pair of binoculars out of his pocket.

"Perfect." I set our snacks out on the table within easy reach. Then Raymond and I settled onto our cushions, binoculars aimed at Isabelle's house.

For a long time we didn't talk. We just watched.

The party had just started. Music blared from outdoor speakers as Isabelle, Katie, Paz, and Lydia splashed in the water. Isabelle's older brother, Martin, staked out his own mini-party near the diving board with Kip and Thea. Isabelle's father lit the grill.

"Hey, Paz!" Martin called. "Where's your sister?"

"You mean Melina?" Paz turned to him, shading her eyes. "She's home watching my little brothers."

"Too bad," Martin said. "I was hoping she'd stop by."

Paz shrugged and went back to practicing handstands in the water. The back door slid open, and two boys swaggered onto the patio. They wore T-shirts with long, baggy board shorts and seemed very sure that wherever they went, girls would be happy to see them.

"Who are they?" Raymond asked.

"Chris and Henry," I replied. "Middle school boys from Isabelle's class."

Chris rubbed his hands together. "Let's get this party started!"

Mr. Barton looked up from the grill. "Hey there, boys."

Chris and Henry nodded politely at Isabelle's dad as if they'd just realized he was there. "Hello, Mr. Barton," they both said. Then they peeled off their shirts and cannonballed into the pool, crying out, "Cowabunga!" The girls screamed and laughed, deflecting the watery fallout with their arms.

Isabelle had boys at her party. Not in the usual way boys go to kids' parties, like when the Mean Boys came to my birthday party last year because Mom forced me to invite them, and then they popped all the balloons and started a food fight. This was different. This was a boy-girl party, the way Thea had boys at her birthday party last year and the boys and girls would disappear for a while and then come back looking flushed and guilty. That kind of boy-girl party.

And Paz was there, perfectly at home. Like she belonged.

"Let's play Marco Polo," Isabelle said. "Katie, you're It." She tied a bandanna over Katie's eyes so she couldn't see. Everyone swam into the deep end of the pool to get away from her.

"Marco!" Katie called.

"Polo!" everyone answered.

Isabelle pulled Paz to her side and whispered to her.

"Marco!" Katie paddled toward the deep end and just missed touching Lydia, who dodged her hands.

"Polo!"

Giggling, Isabelle and Paz climbed out of the pool and perched on the edge. Climbing out of the pool is against the rules in Marco Polo.

"Marco!" Katie called.

Paz and Isabelle leaned out over the water and yelled, "Polo!" When Katie swam toward their voices, her hands only touched cement. Paz and Isabelle tiptoed along the side of the pool, answering "Polo!" and running out of Katie's reach.

"Iz!" Lydia said. "What are you doing?"

Isabelle put her finger to her lips. Lydia didn't say another word, except "Polo."

Katie could have tagged Chris or Henry or Lydia, but she was only interested in going after Paz and Isabelle.

"They're cheating," I muttered.

"They are?" Raymond said. "I was trying to figure out what the heck was going on in that pool."

"You never played Marco Polo before?"

Raymond shook his head. "Once I lived in a house that had a little pool, but the only game we played there was called Dunk the Dork. And I was always the Dork."

Isabelle and Paz kept teasing Katie. Lydia watched and never gave them away. At last Katie gave up and touched Henry on the shoulder. Now he was Marco. She ripped the bandanna off her head just as Paz and Isabelle sprang back into the pool.

"Hey! Were you cheating?" Katie asked.

"No," Isabelle said. "You just couldn't catch us."

Katie looked at Lydia for confirmation. "Iz is a great swimmer" was all Lydia had to say.

"I wonder why nobody is telling on them," I said.

"Because it's Isabelle's party, and she's the boss of it," Raymond said.

But then Martin said, "Iz, you are so cheating. Katie, take it from her brother: You can't trust Isabelle."

Isabelle laughed this off, but Katie looked wounded. She watched Isabelle and followed after her like a puppy.

Isabelle and Paz stayed in the pool while Henry was Marco. He tagged Isabelle, who then became Marco. Within two seconds she tagged Katie. "You're It."

Once Katie was blindfolded, Isabelle beckoned to Paz, and they pulled their trick again. Katie tagged Lydia and yanked the blindfold off before Isabelle and Paz had a chance to get back into the water. I aimed my binoculars at Katie's face and saw it: a stab of pain.

The look of betrayal. It was becoming very familiar to me.

"You *were* cheating. I knew it." Katie dropped the blindfold in the water and climbed out of the pool.

"Katie, where are you going?" Isabelle ran after her.

"I don't want to play anymore." Katie walked fast to her chair, leaving a trail of wet footprints on the cement. "It's no fun if you cheat."

Paz stayed in the pool and watched. She glanced at Lydia, who smiled and shrugged. Paz was so much more quiet and watchful than usual. Like this whole party was a game and she was trying to figure out what the real rules were.

I put my binoculars down and looked at Raymond. He wasn't watching the girls in the pool. He aimed his binoculars at the grill and the table. Isabelle's mom was grilling hamburgers, and her dad was setting down plates. Isabelle's dad passed by her mom on his way back into the kitchen and bumped her playfully with his hip. Raymond sighed.

"What was that?" I asked.

"What?"

"That sigh."

"Nothing. Isabelle's parents seem nice, don't you think?"

"Yeah," I said. "But Isabelle's not. What are you watching the parents for, anyway? That's the boring part."

"Not to me," Raymond said.

"Are you hungry?" I passed him a bag of chips.

"Thanks." He ripped open the bag and ate the chips with one hand while holding his binoculars with the other.

When it was time to eat, Katie tried to sit next to Isabelle, but Isabelle shook her head and said that the seat was saved for Paz. Katie started to sit on Paz's other side, but Lydia slid into that spot before Katie could claim it. There were no seats left except at the other end of the table with the boys, who were too busy gobbling hamburgers to pay attention to her.

By the end of dinner, when it started to get dark, Paz's face was glowing. She was happy, I could tell. Isabelle paid attention to her the whole time, and everyone else did too, because Isabelle led the way. Everyone except Katie, who drooped as the party went on.

"Look how much fun Paz is having," I said to Raymond. My voice felt raggedy. We hadn't talked in a while.

"Yeah." Raymond's binoculars were pointed at me.

"You're not watching the party," I said.

"I'm watching you watch the party."

"But how can you see me when the binoculars are so close?" I asked

"I can see one part of your face at a time. I can see your mouth twitch up or down, or your eyes get wide or squinty."

"But why would you want to see that?" I put my binoculars down.

"You're watching Paz, and I'm watching you. I'm watching you watch Paz. The more you watch her, the sadder you get."

"Because look at her!" I waved my binoculars at the pool. "Isabelle really likes her, and Paz really likes that Isabelle likes her. And I'm not there. And Paz doesn't care. She's having fun without me. We never have fun together anymore."

"So what?" Raymond was still staring at me super close-up through the binoculars. It made me nervous.

"Would you please put those down?" I said. "I can't talk to you like that."

He put them down. "So what if you never have fun with Paz anymore? She's not the only person in the world. I mean, don't you ever have fun with anyone else?"

He fluttered his short blond eyelashes, and I knew he was talking about himself. And I realized I did have fun with him. I was having fun with him that very afternoon, even though I was also in terrible jealous pain over Paz.

But I didn't say it. And I'll always regret that.

The back door slid open, and Melina appeared. "Hey, guys." Her eyes found Martin, Thea, and Kip. Martin headed straight over to her.

"Hey, Melina! Sit down a minute. Want a burger?"

"I came to pick up Paz," Melina said. "Paz, Mami wants you home right now."

"What? But the party just started!" Paz whined.

"Stay here and go for a swim, Melina," Martin said.

"I can't," Melina told him. "Come on, Paz, we have to go. Walk back with us, Thea?"

This was a test. Melina was really asking Thea, "Who do you like best, me or Kip?"

Through my binoculars, I saw Kip tug on the end of Thea's ponytail. "I think I'll stay here and go for a swim," she said.

"Come on, Melina," Paz said. "Let's stay."

"We *can't*." Melina frowned. "Mami's waiting. Kip, walk back with us?"

"I'm going to stay too," Kip said.

I zoomed in on Melina's face. She looked like she was about to cry. She had to babysit her little brothers and sisters instead of having fun with her friends. But that wasn't the only problem. Kip and Thea were standing close together — like they were a team. Like they didn't want to be apart, and not even Melina could make Thea pull away from him.

"Fine," Melina said. "Paz, we're leaving."

She walked back into the house without waiting for Paz. Paz pouted, but she knew her parents would get mad at her if she dawdled. So she got to her feet, said good-bye to everyone, and followed Melina through the sliding door.

The party was breaking up anyway. Lydia's mom stopped by to take her home, and then a man stopped by to pick up Chris and Henry. Thea and Kip went inside the house with Martin. Isabelle's parents cleared the table and put away the food. Isabelle and Katie sat by the pool and dangled their feet in the water as it got dark.

"What's taking your dad so long?" Isabelle asked. "Do you think he forgot to pick you up?"

Katie shrugged. "I don't know. He'll be here soon, I guess."

"He's always late picking you up," Isabelle said. "Ever notice that?"

"He's really busy," Katie said.

A few minutes later a tall man appeared and waved to Katie. "Okay, honey, let's go."

She got up and gathered her things. "Thanks for the party, Isabelle. See you at the pool tomorrow?"

"I don't know. Maybe." Isabelle waved good-bye to Katie but didn't get up from the pool.

"I'd better get home too," I said. I stuffed my things in my backpack and started down the tree house ladder. Raymond scampered down behind me.

We walked down Bailey Street. It was a quiet night. Up ahead of us, Katie and her father turned the corner.

I didn't have to say anything to Raymond. I didn't even have to look at him. We both had the same thought at the same time.

We slowed down and followed Katie home.

She walked a few blocks with her father carrying her tote bag. They didn't talk much. They stopped in front of a low, brick house, dark except for the front porch light, and walked inside.

Raymond and I stopped and watched. A light went on in the living room. Katie's father sat down in a chair and flicked on the TV. We could see its cold blue light on his face. Upstairs, a window lit up. Katie crossed the room. She stopped in front of a small bowl where a lone goldfish swam. She talked to the fish and sprinkled food into the bowl. Then she took the bowl to the window and gazed out past the treetops, into the sky.

I looked at Raymond. Raymond looked at me.

"It's her," he whispered. "*No one loves me except my goldfish.*"

CHAPTER 29
A Plan

I woke up the next morning wondering about my aura. If it was getting blue on the Fourth of July, what color was it now? How much bluer could blue get?

I wish I had the guts to run away.

Run away from what? I wasn't sure, but I understood the feeling.

I pulled open the drawer of my night table and took out my harmonica. It gleamed silvery and shiny in the morning sun.

Raymond had said he didn't have any money. He'd been caught stealing pictures from people's garages, including mine. And he'd admitted stealing Paz's ID.

I had to face facts: He'd probably stolen this harmonica for me.

I played "You Are My Sunshine" one last time. Then I got dressed, put the harmonica in my pocket, and went outside.

Old Donna was parked in Mr. Gorelick's driveway, ready for her weekly wash, but Mr. Gorelick was not around. The garage door gaped open.

I sneaked over there and set the harmonica on top of a workbench.

Good-bye, harmonica. Thanks for the memories.

I went into our garage and put my roller skates on and skated up to the dead-end part of our street to practice. Nobody else was out but I could hear Hugo and Robbie fighting inside the Calderons' house.

The Mean Boys rolled up on their bikes, popping wheelies. "You have to move," Troy told me. "This is our Extreme Bike Stunt Practice Area."

"I was here first," I protested.

"Two against one," David said.

"Paz will be out in a minute," I lied. "Then it will be two against two. And since I was here first, I get to stay."

Troy cupped his ear as if he couldn't hear me. "Did you hear a noise, David? Like a mosquito buzzing?"

"Yeah," David said. "Buzz, buzz, zzzz . . . but I couldn't understand a word."

I rolled my eyes and kept on skating. They started jumping the sidewalk and spinning out as if I wasn't there.

Hugo and Robbie tumbled out of the house, rolling on the grass, fighting over a toy car. Lennie came out with them and sat on the curb. She chomped on some gum and blew a big, green bubble.

"Hey, Lennie," I said. "Curse anybody lately?"

"Ha-ha."

"Where's Paz?" Troy asked. "I thought you said she was coming out to skate."

"Inside," Lennie said. "She's afraid to come out."

"Whoa, because of us?" David crowed. "She's scared of us?"

"Not *you*," Lennie said. "Minty."

Troy flashed me a sizing-up look. "Did Minty gain some kind of superpower I don't know about?"

"Yeah. I can read minds." I leaned close to give him the full effect of my evil grin. "I know all your secrets."

It was a risky thing to say — too close to the truth — but worth it to see Troy's nervous shudder.

"Paz thinks you're mad at her, Mint," Lennie said. The boys, instantly bored, headed off. "And she's barely speaking to me — thanks for telling on me."

"I *am* mad at her. And I warned you I'd tell. Is the curse still on?"

"Still on. Paz has a headache." Lennie wiggled her eyebrows meaningfully. "And lately I've been thinking: What if her tongue swelled up so she couldn't talk?"

"That's harsh." I felt sorry for Paz, even though I was mad at her. I couldn't help it. A voodoo curse is a terrible thing.

Melina marched out of the house. "Minty Mortimer, would you please give your sister a message for me?"

"Sure, Melina."

"Tell her I want my T-shirt back. The one she borrowed from me last spring, with the big, blue heart on it. It's my favorite T-shirt, and she's had it too long."

"Okay."

"Tell her to give it to you, and you can give it to me," Melina said. "Since I never want to speak to her or see her lying face again." She whirled around, hair flying, and marched back into the house. Paz dodged her and limped outside, holding her aching forehead.

"How was Isabelle's party?" I asked, as if I didn't know.

"Okay," Paz said.

"I thought you said it was the best party you've ever been to," Lennie said.

"I thought *you* were going to keep that to your bat-brained self," Paz said.

"Did you see what just happened?" I said. "Melina and Thea are in a terrible fight."

"I know," Paz said. "Melina says she'll never forgive Thea."

"Their friendship is over." Lennie dragged a finger across her throat as if she were slicing it with a knife. "Kaput."

Suddenly, I felt weighed down with sadness, heavy as a drenched shirt. Melina was mad at Thea, I was mad at Paz, Lennie was mad at Paz too, and Paz was mad at Lennie. It was all too much. It had to stop.

"We can't let Thea and Melina's friendship die," I said. "I know why they're fighting, and it's a silly reason."

"I know why they're fighting too," Paz said. "Thea knew Melina liked Kip, but she stole him anyway — right out from under her. Your sister is a bad friend." She crossed her arms and glared at me as if I were a bad friend too.

"Excuse me, but you're the one who's going to parties without me," I snapped. "And making new friends and leaving me all alone at the pool."

Lennie popped a bubble, impressed. "You left Minty all alone at the pool?"

"Well, I —" Paz stammered. "Isabelle wanted to leave, and —"

Lennie peeled a bit of green gum off her cheek. "That's cold."

"I have a plan to make Thea and Melina friends again by the time school starts," I said. This plan had just popped into my head. "But I'll need your help."

Paz turned a wary eye on me. "Is this a trick? Some clever way to get revenge on me?"

"No! I'm not that clever."

"Okay. What's the plan?"

"I call it —" I fumbled for a good name, and came up with: "Operation Annoy Our Sisters. Part One: Annoy Thea. Part Two: Annoy Melina."

"Ooh," Lennie said. "I like it."

"Think about it," I said. "What does Thea do for Melina that no one else will do?"

"Um . . . steal the boys Melina likes?" Paz said.

"No. One thing they have in common is they're both big sisters. What does Melina do when you get on her nerves?" I asked.

"She runs to Thea to whine about it," Paz replied.

"Exactly. That's what Thea does too. Sometimes she complains to Mom and Dad when I annoy her, but they don't want to hear about it. The only person who understands is Melina."

"So?"

"So I'll be as annoying as possible. I'll drive Thea so crazy she'll have talk to Melina — she won't be able to help herself. And if you do the same thing, Melina will have to forgive Thea."

"Even if it doesn't work," Lennie said, "it sounds like fun."

"Hmmm . . ." Paz thought it over. "I have another idea. Part Three: an extra element that will make your plan work even better. But I'll have to recruit Isabelle."

"Isabelle?" I did not like the sound of this at all.

"It won't work unless she helps us," Paz insisted.

"What will she do?" I asked.

"Just trust me," Paz said. "Will you trust me?"

I looked at Paz. We'd been best friends for so long. If I didn't trust her now, what chance would we ever have?

I can't run away from this.

"Go for it," Lennie urged.

"Okay," I said. "It's a team effort. Let's do this."

"Hooray!" Lennie jumped for joy. "Let the torture begin!"

CHAPTER 30
Operation Annoy Thea

I put Operation Annoy Thea into action that very afternoon. I knocked on her bedroom door.

"Don't come in!" she growled. Perfect. She was already in a cranky mood.

"I have a message from Melina for you," I called through the door.

She yanked the door open. "What?" She blocked the entrance to her room, but I slipped past her. I walked straight to her dresser and picked up a seashell from the box of shells she kept there. I picked up one shell, looked at it, touched it a lot, and put it back. Then I picked up another one, looked at it, put it back.

"Well? What's the message?"

"She wants her T-shirt back. The one with the blue heart on it."

"Why doesn't she ask me for it herself?"

"I guess she's not speaking to you for some reason." I picked up Thea's watch, studied it, and made sure to cover the crystal with fingerprints.

"Put that down." Thea snatched the watch away from me and placed it carefully back on the dresser. "Is there anything else?"

"Um . . . yes." I moved on to her bookshelf. I picked up a geode she kept there.

"Well, what? Would you please stop touching my stuff?"

"Sorry. It's an involuntary habit." I opened her closet and tried on a pair of sandals. She practically slammed the door on my foot.

"That's it. Get out of my room," she ordered.

"You're not the boss of me," I taunted.

"My room is my territory, and I'm the boss of my territory," she shot back.

Ooh, I was getting to her. But it wasn't enough. Not yet.

That evening, while Thea was helping Dad fix dinner, I decided to borrow some of her clothes without asking first.

I sneaked into her room — her *territory* — and went through her closet. She had a lot of good clothes, but most of them wouldn't fit me. Not that it really mattered.

Aha — there it was. Her new sundress, the plaid one with spaghetti straps. She'd just bought it and hadn't had a chance to wear it yet. Well, it was about to get broken in.

I put on the dress. It swam on me. The straps were too long. I put a T-shirt under it to make it fit better. The skirt came down past my knees but it twirled in a very satisfying way when I spun around. And it didn't look too bad with my blue Keds.

"Minty! Dinner's ready!" Dad called up the stairs. Showtime.

I walked downstairs and paraded into the kitchen. "Do I smell barbecued chicken? Mmm." Nice and messy.

Thea glared at me. "What are you doing?"

I filled a pitcher with water and started filling the glasses at the table. "What? It's dinnertime. I'm here to eat some barbecued chicken. With my sticky, messy fingers. And then I'm going out later to play Capture the Flag."

"Not in my dress you're not! Why are you wearing my dress?"

I spun around. "It looks pretty good on me, don't you think?"

"Dad!" Thea cried. "Look! She went into my room, which she is not allowed to do, and took that dress out of my closet. And now she's wearing it without my permission!"

Dad carried a bowl of salad to the dinner table. "You two are old enough to settle these fights yourselves."

"But it's not fair!" Thea sputtered. "You know what she was doing earlier? She came into my room and started touching all my stuff!"

Dad grimaced. Thea fell right into my trap. Older sisters hate it when you touch their stuff, but when they try to tell on you, it sounds ridiculous. *What? I didn't break anything.* The perfect crime.

"Thea, I think you're overreacting," Dad said.

"No I'm not!" Thea shrieked. "I'm one hundred percent right, and she's one hundred percent wrong!"

I'm lucky to have such an overdramatic sister. I sat down at my place and smiled what I hoped was an infuriating smile. Mom came in from the patio. "What's going on?"

"Minty is wearing my dress —" Thea began, but Mom held her hand up.

"I thought I should dress up a little for dinner," I said. "I'm just trying to make things civilized around here."

"Mom!" Thea's voice rose to a high squeal. It was an unpleasant sound. Mom winced.

"Stop right there. I don't want to hear another word. Minty, if you've done something wrong to your sister, undo it. Now let's have dinner in peace."

"You little rat!" Thea grabbed me by the arm and dragged me upstairs. "If you won't take that dress off, I'll take it off for you!"

"Careful, you'll rip it!" I warned. I went upstairs and took off the dress. She checked it for damage — amazingly, there was none — and put it back in the closet.

"Never. Wear my clothes. Without asking me. Again. Do you understand?"

I cocked my ear at her as if I were hard of hearing. "What'd you say?"

"You heard me." I swear I saw smoke coming out of her ears. I didn't want her to have a complete heart attack, so I decided to lay off. For the moment.

Operation Annoy Thea was running right on schedule.

CHAPTER 31
David's Secret

The next afternoon, I came home from the pool to find Mom and Wendy having coffee in the kitchen. I almost walked into the middle of a conversation I wasn't sure I was supposed to be hearing. I paused outside the kitchen, listening.

"Everything would be perfect if it weren't for Troy," Wendy was saying. "If Ken holds my hand, Troy karate-chops us apart. Whenever Ken and I have a date, Troy falls to the floor, pretending to have a seizure. He really, really doesn't want his dad to have a girlfriend. I —"

She stopped talking suddenly. There were a few tense seconds of silence while I tried not to breathe. Then Mom called out, "Minty, is that you?"

Caught. So much for getting the real scoop on the Troy situation. I gave up and went into the kitchen.

"Yes, it's me. Hi, Wendy."

"Hi, Minty," Wendy said. "I'm glad you're here. Maybe you can give me some advice on a problem I'm having."

"With Troy?" I sat down at the table and helped myself to a cookie. "His problem is he's a big jerk."

"I think he's just unhappy," Wendy said. "He misses his mother. That's why he acts so . . ." She hesitated.

"Obnoxious?" Mom suggested. "Is that the word you're looking for?"

"He was like that before his mother left," I pointed out.

"Okay, but maybe he was unhappy before she left too," Wendy said. "She must have left for a reason, right? I bet she was unhappy for a long time, and Troy felt it."

It didn't seem fair to let Troy get away with being bad just because he was unhappy. Everybody is unhappy sometimes. But we don't all get a free pass to cause trouble.

As if on cue, Troy and David roared through our backyard like a couple of feuding lions. Troy was throwing tomatoes at David, and David was chasing Troy with a rake.

Wendy sighed. "David isn't what I'd call a good influence. I wonder why *he's* so . . . uh . . ."

"Badly behaved?" Mom suggested.

"If you like," Wendy said. "What do you think, Minty?"

"It's his sisters," I said. "They're always telling him he's stupid, and he believes it. Well, he is *kind of* stupid. Mostly, he can't spell worth a dang, and he's afraid he'll have to be held back a grade."

Wendy and Mom stared at me. "How do you know that?"

"I . . . just know."

"That boy may have behavior problems," Mom said. "But he is not stupid."

"Poor kid!" Wendy shook her head. "Worrying about a thing like that. I know how belittling big sisters can be. I am one myself. I know all the tricks."

"You're a big sister?" I was shocked. She seemed so good-natured and compassionate.

"Yes," Wendy said. "And I regret some of the mean things I did to my little brothers. Not that they didn't deserve it, sometimes." She stared out the window at the boys as they tried to stuff handfuls of grass into each other's mouths.

"Maybe you could help David," I suggested. "You could tutor him on spelling and on big-sister wrangling."

"That's a great idea, Minty," Wendy said. "And if that helps calm him down, maybe he won't be such a bad influence on Troy."

"Yeah . . . maybe." I secretly felt it was an impossible

dream. Also, I was pretty sure Troy was a bad influence on David, not the other way around.

"That's good advice, Minty," Mom said. "Thanks for your help."

"Anytime," I said. "Tell me all your secrets, and I'll take care of them for you."

Just like the Secret Tree, I thought.

Outside, Otis was calling, "Coooorn! Fresh corn! Caaaaaantaloupes . . ."

"Mmm, corn for dinner," Wendy said.

"Stop him, Minty." Mom grabbed her purse off the kitchen counter and looked for her wallet. "We'll be right out."

I ran outside and flagged Otis down. He slowed Esmeralda with a click of his tongue. "What's happening, Minty? Hey, look at that aura. Getting lighter. A little golden around the edges."

"Is that good?"

"It's an improvement, I'll say that. I was getting depressed just looking at you with that dark, muddy aura you were sporting."

"I do feel a little better."

"Say, on my way over here I passed a police car driving fast toward the Witch House. Lights flashing and everything."

"What?"

"I thought you might want to know —"

I took off across the street and into the woods.

"Minty, where are you off to?" Mom called after me.

"I'll be right back!" I yelled over my shoulder, though I didn't know if that was true or not. All I knew was that Raymond might be in trouble.

CHAPTER 32
The Police

Otis was right. A police car was parked in front of the Witch House, its red light warning, *Danger, danger.* I lingered at the edge of the woods, watching to see if it was safe to approach.

Two uniformed officers stood on the rickety front porch, banging on the door. The door opened. I couldn't see who opened it. The police officers flashed their badges and said something to the person in the doorway. They went inside the house. The door closed.

I waited for a few minutes. Nothing happened.

Where was Raymond?

I ran to the model home, darting between abandoned houses like a soldier running for cover. I made it to the front porch and tried the door. It was locked. I rang the bell. It made that stupid formal chime: *ding-dong ding-dong. . . .* I pressed my face to the window so Raymond could see that it was me and not the police.

He opened the door. "Get inside — quick!"

"What's going on?" I was out of breath and could barely speak.

"I don't know." Raymond locked the door behind me. "Don't stand in front of the window."

He ran upstairs, crawled into the pink bedroom, and peered out the window, using the curtain to hide his face. I did the same.

Every few minutes we saw a police officer pass a window of the Witch House. They walked through every room, every floor, searching the place.

"What are they looking for?" I asked.

Raymond didn't answer. But his face was pale, and his hands shook.

I thought about that neighborhood meeting, the rumors about the prowler and the thief. The things Raymond had stolen. Maybe someone had called the police on him. Maybe they were looking for stolen goods —

— like Mr. Gorelick's harmonica. But I gave it back!

I put my hand on Raymond's arm. He took my hand and held it. His palms were sweaty.

At last the Witch House door opened, and the police officers came out. A woman lurked in the doorway. She wouldn't come out. Her hair was ratty, and she was wearing an old nightgown with a hole under the arm.

The Witch Lady.

I'd never gotten a good look at her. No one had, except for Paz, and even then the Witch Lady had been wearing a mask. This was the best view I'd ever had of her, and it wasn't great from this distance. She hung back in the shadow of her house, her face hidden.

The police wandered among the unfinished houses, looking around. They started toward the model home. "Duck!" Raymond ordered.

I ducked and held my breath. I waited to hear their footsteps on the porch, the doorbell ring, the door opening, their steps on the stairs. . . .

The front door rattled. And rattled again. There was a pause. Raymond and I stayed perfectly still, eyes locked on each other.

After what felt like forever, I cautiously lifted my head and peeked out the window. Both officers got into the police car and drove away.

"It's okay," I told Raymond. "We're safe now."

Raymond rolled over on the carpet and shut his eyes. "That was close."

"Are you in some kind of trouble?" I asked.

Raymond took a deep breath. "It's a big mistake. That's all."

He refused to say another word about it.

"If the police get you, I promise I'll tell them what a good person you are," I said. "I'll testify at your trial. I'll tell them you're innocent. Whatever you need."

Raymond looked at me sideways, like he didn't believe me. Which broke my heart. Because I meant it. I'd do anything to help him.

Invisible or not, he was my friend.

He checked for signs of the police one last time. They were definitely gone, and the door to the Witch House was closed. We went downstairs to the living room. He picked up his harmonica and played a slow, sad song.

"That's beautiful," I said.

He paused. "I'll teach you how to play it. Where's your harmonica?"

My heart nearly stopped. This was the question I'd been dreading. He watched me, waiting for my answer.

"I don't have it," I confessed.

"Oh. Well, bring it next time." Raymond played a *tweedleedeet!*

"I can't," I said. "I . . . don't have it anymore."

"What do you mean? You gave it away?"

"Sort of."

"But I gave it to you. It was a present."

"I know, but . . ." I didn't want to tell him that I returned it to Mr. Gorelick. But Raymond was waiting for an explanation. "Raymond, was it stolen?"

"No. I didn't steal it."

"Mr. Gorelick said someone stole a harmonica out of his garage. And I knew you had taken things from other people's garages, like my school picture, and Kip's —"

"So you think I stole the harmonica?"

"Well, I —"

"I didn't steal it."

"I'm sorry. I was afraid it was stolen," I said. "So I put it back in Mr. Gorelick's garage."

"What?"

I didn't want to repeat it, so I stayed silent.

"I gave it to you," he said.

"I know."

"So get it back."

"I can't. It's not mine. It's Mr. Gorelick's."

He dropped his harmonica on the floor. "I don't believe it. You think I'm a thief."

"No, not really," I said. "I just — I knew — well, I did catch you —"

"I thought we were friends." He ran upstairs.

"Raymond, wait!" I ran after him. I found him in his room, the room with the boats and the anchors, lying on the bottom bunk, clutching a black stuffed animal.

"You think I'm a thief," he repeated.

"I'm sorry. I was wrong! I don't think you're a thief. I think you're a great friend! I really like you."

"You gave away my present."

"I'll ask Mr. Gorelick about it," I promised. "Maybe I can get it back —"

I looked more closely at the stuffed animal he was holding. It looked very familiar.

It was a cat.

Marcella.

"Where did you get that cat?" I asked.

"It's mine." He held it tighter, like he was scared I'd try to take it away from him.

"I know. But where did you get it?"

"I didn't steal it, if that's what you're thinking. My mother gave it to me."

His mother . . . the Witch Lady.

She'd ripped Marcella off of Paz's shoulder. And she gave the cat to her son.

To Raymond.

Lennie wanted Marcella back. It was the only way she'd take the curse off of Paz.

But Raymond thought Marcella was his. From his mother. From the way he held her, he'd never give her up — especially not to me, the horrible girl who gave away his harmonica and thought he was a thief.

I could snatch Marcella away from him and run. I could run all the way home and give the cat to Lennie and save Paz.

I could have done that. But I didn't have the heart.

I reached for Marcella. Raymond jerked her away. I reached farther and touched her fur.

I petted her.

He rolled over and pressed his face into the pillow.

"Raymond, please forgive me."

He didn't move. He didn't say a word.

I sat beside him, waiting, listening. The house was quiet. Raymond's smell was stronger now, a mixture of mud and bologna and ketchup and glue. The paint and carpet smells had faded away. The house belonged to Raymond.

Through the window, I could see the second floor of the Witch House. The Witch Lady stood in front of a torn screen, staring out. She had a hard face. I couldn't tell if she was angry or very, very sad.

Downstairs, the refrigerator clicked and started to hum. There was no other noise in the house.

"Don't you get lonely here, all by yourself?" I asked.

"Go away."

It sounds like fun to have a whole house to yourself. But in real life, I don't think it is.

From the other side of the woods, I heard the ship's bell faintly clanging, almost as if Mom sensed I was thinking about her and decided to call me home.

"I've got to go," I told Raymond. "But I'll be back another day. And you can always come find me if you want. You know where I live."

He didn't move. I hated to leave this way, but I had to.

Outside, the sunny day had darkened. The air smelled like metal. Rain was coming. The wind picked up. I hurried through the woods, hoping to get home before the storm started.

A gust of wind pushed me along. The wind sang in the

treetops. As I passed the Secret Tree, I thought I heard the spirit of Crazy Ike cackling.

Not all of the secrets had been put in the tree. There were some that we still held on to because they were too hard to let go.

Chapter 33
The New Recruit

The rain stopped after dinner. I went over to Paz's house to see how Operation Annoy Our Sisters was coming along on the Melina side.

Lennie let me in. I was seized with the urge to blurt out, "I saw Marcella!" But I held my tongue. What good would that do? I couldn't bring myself to take Marcella away from Raymond, so Lennie would only get mad at me. Then maybe she'd make a voodoo doll of me, and I didn't want that.

I'd have to find another way to convince Lennie to stop the curse. So many feuds! When I thought about it too much, I got dizzy.

"Paz is in our room," Lennie said, leading me upstairs. "And she's not alone."

"What do you mean? Who's here?"

"You'll see."

I walked into their bedroom, and there sat Paz and Isabelle, painting each other's toenails dark blue, the color of a bruise.

"Hey, Minty." Paz's voice sounded welcoming and cheerful, but her face looked a little nervous.

Isabelle looked up briefly and said hi before focusing her concentration on Paz's left big toe. It wasn't the warmest welcome I'd ever gotten. I guess I just had to pretend I didn't know she'd had a pool party and didn't invite me.

"Should I leave?" I asked.

"No! Why?" Paz capped the nail polish bottle and gave it a shake.

"Sit down." Lennie made room for me on her bed. "If you can stand the fumes."

"I just stopped by to see how things were going with Melina," I said. "Is she still mad at Thea?"

"Oh, yeah," Paz said. "But she *hates* me. I wrote a parody of one of her songs."

"It really showcases the weaknesses in Melina's song-writing style," Lennie said.

"Plus I left a hard-boiled egg in her closet, which she didn't notice until it rotted," Paz said.

"And I threatened to cut her hair in her sleep," Lennie added. "She'll be begging for mercy soon."

"My part of the plan is coming along too," Isabelle said.

"What exactly is your part of the plan?" I asked.

"My brother, Martin," Isabelle replied. "He has a huge crush on Melina."

"He does?" Now that Isabelle mentioned it, I remembered how Martin had asked Paz if Melina was coming to the pool party, and how he'd perked up when Melina came to pick up Paz.

"Huge," Isabelle confirmed. "But he's too shy to tell her."

"That's Part Three of the plan," Paz said. "If Melina has a boyfriend of her own, she won't care so much about Thea and Kip."

"And she'll forgive Thea more easily," Isabelle said.

"Very clever." I warmed up to Isabelle, slightly, now that she was finally making herself useful.

"I just have to convince him to work up the courage to tell Melina he likes her," Isabelle said. "That's going to be the hard part."

"You work on him, and we'll keep annoying our sisters," I said. "Between the four of us, this plan has got to work."

"We make a pretty good team," Isabelle said.

I wasn't ready to go that far. Isabelle's callous behavior was still fresh in my mind. But I was willing to give her a chance, if it would help make Thea and Melina friends again.

One chance. But if she did anything mean, or had any cruel tricks up her sleeve, that was the end. Paz could have her.

CHAPTER 34

Summertime's the Worst

"Look, Dad. I just made this poster for my room." I brought my latest art project outside to the patio, where Dad was listening to the Orioles game on the radio, and Thea was reading in the sun. I'd spent the morning making a giant roller derby poster. I drew a picture of myself in uniform, scowling and hip-checking a skater from the opposing team. Across the top I wrote in large, red letters: *The Catonsville Nine, starring Minty Fresh!* "Aren't you proud of me?"

Dad studied the poster carefully. He'd always been a big supporter of my roller derby career. "Very sharp, Minty. I love the colors — where did you get such a bright red? And those pastels —" He leaned closer and touched a powdery light blue I'd used for the background. A bit of blue came off on his finger. "It's not paint, and it's not colored pencil. . . ."

"No, I didn't use either of those." I grinned. "I used a completely new medium this time."

Something mischievous in my voice must have caught Thea's attention. She looked up and glanced at the poster.

Then she looked again. Then she stood up and swiped her finger through the black line around the helmet. "Hey . . . Minty, what is this?" .

"It's — it's, um . . ." Now that I'd gotten the attention I wanted, I was a little afraid of the consequences. "It's this, um, stuff I found that's really fun to draw with —"

"Stuff you found in my room!" Thea growled. "This is my makeup!"

"What?" Dad looked at the poster again. "You drew this with makeup?"

Thea ran upstairs to check. A minute later, her scream shattered the peaceful summer morning.

"Minty! I'm going to kill you!" She stormed back outside. "Dad! She used my makeup to make this stupid poster!"

"Minty! Is that true?"

What was I going to say? I knew this would make Thea crazy. I opened my mouth, hoping some kind of butt-saving answer would come out. And my good luck saved me. Dad's cell phone buzzed. He was on call that day.

"Just a second." Dad held up his hand to us, to put us on hold while he took the call. He stood up and paced while he talked. "Yes? Yes. Okay. I'll be right there." He hung up. "Sorry, girls, they need me at the hospital. We can take this up later. Minty — do not touch your sister's things without permission, okay?"

Thea groaned and stamped her foot in frustration. "Is that all you're going to do? You're not going to yell at her or punish her or anything?"

Dad went inside to change his shoes. "Thea, I don't have time for this right now. Take it up with your mother when she gets home."

"You never do anything to her! She's the most annoying person on the face of the earth, and she gets away with murder!" Thea cried.

Dad grabbed his car keys, kissed her on the forehead, kissed me on the forehead, said, "Be good," and left for work.

Thea's eyes burned into me. I was the peskiest little sister in the world, and nobody cared. She had to find somebody to take her side or she would explode.

"I'm in charge until Mom comes home," she said. "I'm going outside. Do not leave the house."

She went out the front door. Two doors down, Kip was in his driveway with his head under the hood of his car. "Kip!" She sprinted toward him. "Kip, listen to this!"

I went outside and sat on the front steps to watch, disobeying her once again. Farther down the street, just beyond Kip's house, Paz was setting up a microphone and a beat box in her front yard. Lennie filmed everything she did on Paz's phone. I gave them a conspiratorial little wave. They waved back.

Kip came up for air, smiling and smeared with grease.

"Thea! Want to help me change some spark plugs?"

She ignored him. "You know what Minty did? She drew a poster using my makeup. All my favorite lipsticks, eye shadows, pencils — ruined!"

Kip's smile faded. I chuckled to myself. I could tell that this was a problem he did not understand.

"She's always going in my room and *touching* all my stuff!" Thea knew she was losing him, but she had to make somebody understand how hard her life as a big sister was. "She wears my clothes, she has no sense of boundaries —"

"Aw, come on," Kip said. "She's a nice kid."

Thea's expression darkened ominously. Kip had not said the right thing.

"Well, I guess you could get back at her by wearing *her* clothes," Kip suggested lamely.

Thea was practically tearing her hair out in frustration. "Her clothes are little-kid clothes! They don't fit me, and I wouldn't want to wear them if they did. And besides, half of them are hand-me-downs from me — I already wore them!"

Kip dove back into his car's engine. "Don't you understand?" Thea cried.

"Sure," he muttered. "I get it. Casey can be a real brat too." But he didn't really get it. Because if he did, he would have been outraged. His little sister, Casey, was quiet and not very bratty at all.

Down at the Calderons' house, Paz's microphone gave a squeal of feedback. She started the beat box and began to sing. Lennie circled Paz with the camera on her phone.

"Hey hey, go away, it's a muggy summer day.
Beat beat, smell my feet, they get stinky in the heat.
Why why, do I cry, I got something in my eye, yo.
Summertime's the worst time, summertime's the
worst . . ."

"Hey," Thea said. "That's Melina's song. Paz is making fun of it!"

"It's pretty good." Kip bopped to the beat without really listening to the words.

Melina came running out of the house, screen door slapping shut behind her. "What do you think you're doing?" She snatched the microphone away from Paz and switched off the amplifier.

Paz played innocent. "I want to be creative like you, so I wrote a song."

"And I'm making the video to post on YouTube," Lennie added.

"Don't worry, we'll give you full songwriting credit," Paz said.

"You mean you wrote a parody of my song! You're making fun of me in front of the whole neighborhood!"

Melina self-consciously glanced toward Kip and Thea. Then she grabbed the camera from Lennie. "The whole world!"

I had to get closer now, to see and hear everything. I walked down the street to Kip's house. Thea caught Melina's eye. I saw it — a flash of sympathy. Here were two girls who understood each other. Two girls with the same problem: bratty little sisters. Two best friends.

Melina ran toward Thea. Thea ran to meet her. It was just like in old movies when two lovers run to each other in slow motion. Kip barely looked up from his car.

"I can't believe what Paz just did to you," Thea said. "But wait until you hear what Minty did!"

"What? Tell me everything, and then we'll make a plan to get back at them."

I joined Paz and Lennie on the grass while Thea and Melina released all their big-sister tension to each other. At last, someone who understood.

"Good job," I said to Paz and Lennie.

"Same to you," Paz said.

"They're speaking again," Lennie said. "It's a start."

"What about the revenge they're planning?" I said. "How bad do you think it will be?"

"I don't think they're ever going to get around to it," Paz said. "They'll be too busy with their new boyfriends."

"Boyfriendzzz?"

"Martin finally told Melina he likes her," Lennie said. "She doesn't care about Kip anymore."

"So now we can stop torturing our big sisters," Paz said.

"Whoa — let's not get crazy," I said. "I can't stop cold turkey. Annoying Thea is part of my lifestyle."

Paz laughed her good-old-Paz laugh. I felt like we were friends again, the way we used to be. Or almost the way we used to be.

"Hey," she said. "Want to go to the pool later with me and Isabelle?"

"Sure." I felt happy. Things with Paz might not be exactly like they once were. But maybe they'd get even better.

"What about me?" Lennie asked.

"Well, you belong to the pool, so I can't stop you from going," Paz conceded.

Lennie scowled. Her face said, *You'll be sorry.*

An hour later, Paz's tongue swelled up.

CHAPTER 35
Raymond's Secret

Dad gave Paz an antihistamine that reduced the swelling in her tongue. He said it was probably some kind of allergic reaction. I knew better.

Paz was okay for now. But Lennie wasn't fooling around.

It was time to get Marcella, I decided, before Lennie took the curse too far.

I set off for Raymond's house.

On the way I found a new secret:

I like Melina.

Well, duh. Martin Barton for sure. I just hoped Raymond had a picture of Martin ready to be captioned.

I rang the doorbell — *ding-dong ding-dong* — but no one answered. I listened for any sound in the house. Maybe Raymond was hiding. I knew he was very mad at me.

The house was silent. I knocked. "Raymond, please let me in!"

Nothing.

I knocked again. "I'm sorry about the harmonica! I'll get a new one!"

Silence.

"I've got a new secret to show you!"

When he didn't answer, I tried the doorknob. It was unlocked.

I went inside.

Raymond wasn't home. I checked every room. He wasn't there.

Strange, I thought. *I wonder where he is.*

Marcella sat stuffed in a corner of the living room couch. I picked her up. I could take her back to Lennie right now. It would be so easy. She would lift the curse off of Paz, and that problem would be solved.

I put Marcella back and sat down with the secret notebook. Raymond had taken a Polaroid of Martin talking to Kip in front of Kip's car. I pasted *I like Melina* under his picture. Very satisfying.

I paged through the book, looking at all the secrets we had matched to people in the neighborhood over the summer. Troy and David, Thea and Melina, Lennie and Katie . . .

I decided to invite them all to my birthday party, Katie and Lydia and Isabelle too. Even the Mean Boys. And Raymond, if he would come. I'd always had just one best friend, Paz. But now I had a whole circle of friends, and it was growing all the time.

I turned to the page that showed a rather sour-faced picture of Lennie over her secret: *I put a curse on my enemy. And it's working.*

I picked up Marcella. Where was Raymond? I couldn't just steal Marcella from him without an explanation. I went to the kitchen window and looked out at the muddy yards of the unfinished houses in the new development. I looked at the fading Witch House. And there he was.

He stood inside the Witch House, near the living room window, crying. The Witch Lady towered over him, saying something to him.

Then Raymond threw his arms around her waist, clinging to her. He sobbed. At first, the Witch Lady didn't do anything. She stood still and frozen, arms at her sides, as if she were afraid to touch him. He gripped her tighter, pressed his face into her belly. She wouldn't move.

Raymond didn't let go. He would never let go. At last the Witch Lady started to cry too. She fell onto her knees and wrapped Raymond in her arms and held him tight.

I couldn't take Marcella away from him. I left the model house and walked home through the woods.

CHAPTER 36
The Harmonica

"Hey, Minty!" Mr. Gorelick was in his driveway, polishing Old Donna. "Is this yours?"

A shiny object flashed in his hand. I walked over to see it. It was the harmonica Raymond had given me.

"I found this tin sandwich in my garage the other day," Mr. Gorelick said. "Don't you have one just like it?"

"I did, but I lost it." I took the harmonica, glad to feel its cool weight in my hand again.

"Wonder how it got here," Mr. Gorelick said. "Maybe that Man-Bat is playing tricks on us. Ha-ha."

"Isn't it yours? I thought your harmonica was stolen."

"It wasn't," Mr. Gorelick said. "I just misplaced it. Actually, my darn wife hid it from me."

"Oh." So Raymond hadn't stolen my gift after all. I felt terrible.

"This one's mine." He held up a large, black harmonica and blew a loud riff on it. "It's a Suzuki Fire Breath. Judy says the sound of it scares Kelly. I don't know how she can tell — all that dog does is pant and sniffle through her tiny little nose." He sighed. "Course I love her like a child, but a dog's not really a child. And someday I'd love to have somebody in this house who's on my side when it comes to harmonica playing." He played a few bars of "You Are My Sunshine." "Isn't that beautiful?"

"Sure is," I said. I put my harmonica to my lips and played along.

Mr. Gorelick grinned. "Now where did you learn that?"

"A friend taught me."

He played the song again, and I played with him. Mrs. Gorelick stuck her head out the window and cried, "What's that racket? Oh — hello, Minty."

"Hi, Mrs. Gorelick. We're playing a duet."

"Okay. Well . . . okay." She shut the window. Mr. Gorelick laughed and said, "Let's play it again."

We played it over and over until we got it just right. The whole time I was thinking of Raymond, and how much he would have enjoyed it. I couldn't wait to tell him I got my harmonica back.

I just hoped he'd forgive me for losing it in the first place.

First chance I got I ran through the woods to find Raymond. As I came near the other side a red light flashed in my eyes. My skin prickled. I had a bad feeling.

Two police cars were parked in front of the Witch House. The Witch Lady was shrieking and crying on the front porch. Two police officers subdued her. A woman in a business suit led Raymond to one of the cars and helped him into the backseat.

Raymond was under arrest! The police had finally caught up with him.

All those things the neighbors had said before the Fourth of July Parade — about thefts, and break-ins, prowlers, voodoo curses, mysterious illnesses, and Man-Bats . . . someone must have called the police — and somehow they blamed Raymond.

But none of those things were his fault. I was the prowler. I was the Man-Bat. I was the one who stole everyone's secrets.

Raymond was getting into trouble for me.

"Wait!" I sprinted out of the woods, waving my arms. "Wait! You're making a terrible mistake!"

A police officer stopped me before I could reach Raymond. The Witch Lady was screaming like crazy, and the two officers were trying to get her to stay still. Raymond sat quietly in the car with wet eyes, holding Marcella tight.

"You're making a mistake," I told the policewoman. "Raymond is innocent. He didn't steal Mr. Gorelick's harmonica." I waved the harmonica so Raymond could see it. "Raymond, look! I got my harmonica back. I know you didn't steal it."

"What are you talking about?" the officer asked.

"Raymond didn't steal anything. Well, nothing valuable, anyway. And I was the one who was spying on my sister when she was babysitting. I'm the one she thought was a prowler! It's all my fault. You have to let him go."

The police officer blinked at me, baffled. "Miss, I don't know anything about a prowler or babysitting. This is a social services matter. I'm afraid I can't say any more."

The other two officers dragged the Witch Lady into the second police car and shut the door. I tried to go to Raymond, but the first officer blocked my way.

"Where are you taking him?" I demanded.

"Don't worry," the officer said. "He's going someplace where he'll be safe. Everything will be okay now."

Raymond didn't look okay. He was crying. The woman in the business suit put her arm around him and spoke quietly to him. He refused to look at her.

The officers got into their car and backed up. Raymond waved to me, a sad little wave. I was glad to see he wasn't wearing handcuffs. I waved back, then blew on the harmonica: *ffflllleeeet! ffflllloooot.*

The two police cars drove off, lights flashing, leaving me behind to wonder what in the world had just happened.

Raymond had made me promise not to tell anyone about him. But this was an emergency. He was in trouble. He needed help. And the only way to get help was to reveal his secret.

I had no choice.

CHAPTER 37
The Witch Lady's Story

Dad came home from work in time for dinner that night. He sat at the table and said, "Here's what I found out."

After the police captured Raymond, I ran home and told Mom and Thea everything. Thea was shocked to hear that the Witch Lady had a child. Mom was shocked to hear that I had a friend she'd never heard of before. We called Dad at work, and he promised to find out what was going on. He had a friend at the hospital who was a social worker and would know what to do.

"Your friend Raymond Delmore Junior was a runaway," Dad said now. "The state social services had sent him to live with a foster family. He didn't like it, so he ran away. The police suspected that he ran home to his mother, Jean Delmore —"

"The Witch Lady?" I said.

"That's her."

"He didn't really live with her," I said. "He had his own house. The model home in the new development."

"I guess that's where he hid when the police came looking for him," Dad said.

"But if she's his mother, why couldn't he stay with her?" I asked.

"She's sick, too sick to take good care of Raymond. A social worker got an anonymous tip and found him locked out of the house one day. It was March, very cold, and Raymond's mother didn't open the door because she was asleep — so heavily asleep she couldn't wake up."

An anonymous tip . . . I thought of Otis.

"What if they knocked on the door harder?" I asked. "What if they knocked really, really hard? Maybe she would've woken up."

Dad shook his head. "She didn't, though. And she locked Raymond out more than once. She probably didn't mean to. I think she just forgot about him. He wasn't safe, living with her."

"So they took him to a foster home to live with people who could take care of him better," Mom said.

"But he ran away from them," I said. "He didn't like them."

"No, he wasn't happy there," Dad said. "And he missed his mother."

"So what's going to happen now?" I asked. "If they send him back to the foster family, he'll just run away again."

Dad frowned. "He's at the children's home, waiting to be placed with a new foster family. His mother is going to stay in the hospital for a while. She's going to try to get better."

"He was doing okay at the model home," I said. But even as I was saying it, I knew it wasn't true. I remembered how empty and lonely the model home felt. How much he loved his secret notebook of friends, friends who didn't even know he existed. How he and his mother cried and held each other tight.

Raymond needed real family and real friends.

"Could we be Raymond's foster family?" I asked. "He could live with us!"

Mom and Dad exchanged one of those *How do we break it to her?* glances. "We don't have an extra bedroom for him," Mom said. "You would have to move into Thea's room."

"What? No way," Thea protested. "I'm not sharing my room with Miss Touchy-Fingers."

I wasn't dying to share a room with her, either, but I was desperate to help Raymond. "What if someone else in the neighborhood could take him?"

"It's possible, I guess," Dad said. "Do you have someone in mind?"

I did. I knew the perfect family for Raymond. If only it could all work out.

CHAPTER 38
Happy Birthday to Me

My birthday is on August 27, at the end of summer. Time to wrap up summer activities, take a last swim, savor those last lazy days. Time to get ready for the new school year. Time to turn eleven.

I held my party at the roller rink like I'd always planned, and I was glad. Mom and Dad gave me knee pads and a mouth guard for my birthday, so I had a chance to try them out. Paz gave me a new roller derby jersey with MINTY FRESH on the back, so I wore that too. She had a matching jersey made for herself that said PAX A. PUNCH.

Thea and Melina skated around and around, holding hands with Kip and Martin. Wendy and Mr. Rogers held hands too. So did Mom and Dad. It was a big lovefest. David and Troy buzzed around, threatening to knock people down but never quite daring to.

Raymond came to the party too. His new foster family thought it would be the perfect time to introduce him to the neighbors. Of course, Raymond already knew all about them, especially their secrets.

While Isabelle and Lydia practiced their twirls, Katie skated up to me and said, "I like roller derby. I don't know many tricks, though."

"Why don't we practice together?" I said. "I don't know many skills either, but it's easier to learn with a partner."

She smiled. "Thanks! I'd love that." Then she speed-skated around the track so fast I knew she'd be a natural.

Paz caught up to me and linked her arm with mine. Isabelle and Lydia joined the chain, and Katie too.

"Paz, will you get me one of those cool roller derby jerseys like you and Minty have?" Isabelle asked.

"Sure," Paz said. "What's your derby name?"

"I don't know yet," Isabelle said. "I'll have to think about it."

"What about Dizzy Izzy?" I suggested. "Or Isabellbottoms?"

"Isabelly-ache," Katie said.

"Isabelly-flop," I added. "You're lucky, Isabelle — you've got a lot of names to choose from."

"Yeah, I guess so." Isabelle looked as if she regretted bringing this subject up.

"Hey, look — there are five of us." I gazed down the line of girls linked arm in arm. "That's just enough to field a team."

"Yeah!" Katie said. "We could start our own junior squad."

"The Catonsville Crashers," Lydia said.

"I like it," Paz said.

"I love it!" I said.

"Happy birthday, Minty," Paz said.

All the girls surrounded me and shouted, "Happy birthday!" We piled our fists one on top of the others and yelled, "Let's go!" We were turning into a team already.

I skated over to the sidelines where Raymond wobbled on his rented skates. I took him by the hand and pulled him onto the track. Paz took his other hand, and we towed him along with us until he got the hang of it.

Once all the guests had arrived, Mr. Gorelick played some chords on the organ — *taran-tarah!* — and stood up to make an announcement. "My dear friends, I would like to introduce you to a new member of our happy group, Raymond Delmore Junior. He's going to be living with Judy and me for a while. We're so glad to have him, and I hope you'll make him welcome."

Everyone clapped, me loudest of all. Raymond would be living next door to me! And Mr. Gorelick would have someone to play harmonica duets with. Mrs. Gorelick gave Raymond a hug. Raymond blushed, but he looked happy.

The Gorelicks invited everyone over to their house for a post-skating barbecue. They hung a big sign over their front door that said HAPPY BIRTHDAY, MINTY, AND

WELCOME, RAYMOND and the whole neighborhood was there to meet him.

"There's the birthday girl." Otis gave me a free watermelon as a birthday gift. "Your aura is looking wonderful today — silver and gold."

"Thanks, Otis." I did feel as if I were radiating a happy glow.

"And, Raymond, my man." Otis shook Raymond's hand. "Very glad to see you're staying in the area. These are good people. Here's a welcome watermelon for you."

"Thank you. I'm glad too." Raymond grinned and sagged under the weight of the watermelon. We put them on the picnic table to share with everyone.

Mr. Rogers and Wendy arrived, still holding hands. Troy trailed after them, looking sour.

"Mr. Rogers looks thinner," Raymond said.

He *did* look thinner. I guess Troy gave up on sabotaging his diet. His plan wasn't going to work anyway — Wendy liked Mr. Rogers whether he was chubby or slim.

David Serrano ran up to Wendy and practically jumped into her arms, he looked so happy to see her. She was tutoring him in writing and also in sister wrangling. "Wendy! I need your advice. Connie and DeeDee are calling me Diet Food for Zombies again."

"Diet Food for Zombies?" Mr. Rogers said. "What does that mean?"

"Slim pickings in the brains department," Troy informed him.

"Here's what you do," Wendy told David. "Ignore them. Pretend like it doesn't bother you. That drives big sisters crazy."

"But what if that doesn't work?" David asked.

"If that doesn't work, say something like 'Well, that means one of us will survive the Zombie Apocalypse, and it's not going to be you.'"

David laughed, but Troy stayed stone-faced.

"Mmm, watermelon." Wendy headed for the picnic table, where Dad was slicing up the watermelons with surgical precision. "Let's go get some." Mr. Rogers followed her.

"Why are you being nice to her?" Troy hissed at David. "She's Troy Rogers's Enemy Number One."

"I think she's cool," David said. "You're lucky she's your dad's girlfriend. You could have ended up with a wicked stepmother instead — like one of my sisters. Or the Witch Lady!"

David didn't realize what he was saying. He didn't know that the Witch Lady was Raymond's mother. I glanced at Raymond, but he didn't flinch. I don't think he thinks of his mother as the Witch Lady. To him she's just his mother.

"Wendy is not my mother," Troy said. "I want my mother back."

"My mother went away too," Raymond said. "That's why I'm here."

David and Troy stared at him. I waited for Troy to say something mean, but he didn't.

"Do you know where she is?" Troy asked. "Aren't you going to try to get her back?"

"I can't get her back yet," Raymond said. "I have to wait until she's ready."

Troy thought this over. Then he said, "Do you like Super Soakers? Because I have a lot of them. Maybe you could come over one day and we'll talk about Super Soakers. And shoot them too."

Raymond hesitated. He knew what kind of boy Troy was. But he said okay because he is kind. And, I think, because he knew Troy needed a friend.

Mr. Jack walked over from his house with two goldfish, each in its own plastic bag. "For the birthday girl." He gave me one of the bags. "And welcome to the neighborhood." He gave the other fish to Raymond.

"Thanks, Mr. Jack." I ran home to put my annual birthday goldfish in the bowl with last year's fish, Zuzu. When I got back to the party, Raymond was gone.

"Where's Raymond?" I asked Paz.

"He went up to his room with Lennie. They're going to decide where to put the goldfish."

Oh, no — Marcella! "I'll be right back." I ran inside the house and up to Raymond's new room.

When I got there, Raymond was setting the goldfish bowl on his dresser. "I think I'll name him Popeye," he said. "Because his eyes are kind of bulgy."

"I named mine Man-Fish, but that's me," Lennie said.

Mrs. Gorelick had put up new wallpaper for Raymond, a pattern of boats and anchors. The bedspread was navy blue, decorated with a boat pillow. It was almost like the model home, only better, and the bed was real. And on top of the bed, leaning against the wall, sat Marcella.

As soon as I saw her, Lennie noticed her too. She gasped and reached for the toy cat. "Hey! That's —"

She stopped and looked at Raymond. I could see her mind working. She knew he was the Witch Lady's son. She was guessing where he must have gotten Marcella from.

Oh, no, Lennie, I thought. *Don't take Marcella away from Raymond.*

"That's what?" Raymond picked up Marcella and hugged her.

"That's . . . I used to have a cat just like that." Lennie watched him with wide, wet eyes.

"My mother gave him to me. I haven't given him a name yet."

"I think he looks like a *her*," Lennie said. "Can I hold her for a second?"

"Sure." Raymond handed Marcella to her. Lennie hugged the cat and picked at a sticky spot on her fur.

"Why don't you name her Marcella?" I said. "Don't you think she looks like a Marcella?"

Lennie smiled at me and gave the cat back to Raymond.

"Okay," Raymond said. "I'll call her Marcella."

"Take good care of her." Lennie swallowed hard.

"I will," Raymond promised.

We settled Raymond's goldfish and went back to the barbecue.

"That was nice of you to let Raymond keep Marcella," I told Lennie. "I'm sure he'll let you visit her whenever you want."

"I — I guess I don't need her anymore," Lennie said. "Raymond loves her. I'm glad she has a good home."

"Does that mean the curse is off?" I asked.

"The curse is off," Lennie said. "Paz can now live the rest of her life curse-free."

I ran across the yard to tell Paz the good news.

Chapter 39
My Book of Friends

As the night grew dark and the party wound down, Raymond took me to his new room and presented me with a rectangle wrapped in comics.

"I haven't given you your birthday present yet," he said.

"Thank you, Raymond." I opened the card first. Raymond had made it himself. It was a drawing of me and him, standing in front of the model home. Inside it said, *Happy birthday to my best friend — Raymond.*

I tore open the wrapping paper. Inside was the secret notebook of friends. "For me?"

He nodded. "I have real friends now. And anyway, the book is finished. Look."

I opened the book and turned the pages. We'd matched up all the secrets with pictures of people we knew, each secret underlining a picture like a caption in a yearbook. Some secrets were decorated with gold stars.

"The gold stars stand for problems we fixed," Raymond told me.

There was Thea's school picture with the caption:

When I'm babysitting, after the kids are asleep, I snoop through the parents' drawers and closets.

Under a picture of Melina playing the guitar, he'd pasted:

I'm in love with Kip Murphy.

Then Martin Barton:

I like Melina.

Next came David Serrano with his squirt rifle.

Im so stoopid. Im affraid something is rong with my brane. But I dont want anywon to find out or theyll kep me back.

Troy had two secrets under his snarling picture.

I'm secretly sabotaging my dad's diet shake by putting cream and sugar in it. He keeps saying he can't believe a diet shake could taste so good! And wondering why he isn't losing weight. But I don't want him to. I have my reasons.

I know where Wendy's cat is. And I'm not telling.

"I think Troy will start to like Wendy soon," Raymond said. "Once he sees that a family can have lots of different people in it."

I just want people to like me.

We'd put that one under Isabelle's picture. But, really, it could have gone with anyone. Secrets can always apply to more than one person, as I'd found.

We assigned this one to Kip:

I wish I had the guts to run away.

We figured that was why he loved his car so much — because he could use it to escape. It couldn't have been Raymond's, because Raymond *had* run away. But I didn't think he'd be running away anymore.

There was our new friend Katie Park.

No one loves me except my goldfish.

And Paz's, which she could have shared with Thea:

I'm betraying my best friend in a terrible way.

Lennie didn't have a gold star.

I put a curse on my enemy. And it's working.

"We can put a star next to Lennie's secret now," I said. "She promised to stop cursing Paz."

Raymond grabbed his box of stars and starred Lennie's secret.

On the last page was a picture of me. Underneath, it said:

BEST FRIEND, MINTY MORTIMER.
SECRET: **I don't want to grow up. Ever.**

That one didn't have a star either.

"How did you know this was mine?" I asked.

"Because I know you," Raymond said.

"We can put a star on this one too," I said. "Because I changed my mind." I wasn't scared of middle school anymore. Paz and Raymond would be there with me, and Isabelle, Katie, and Lydia too. Even Troy and David didn't bother me so much. I had a whole roller derby squad's-worth of middle school friends.

One secret was still loose.

I made a special surprise lunch for my friend.

"Don't forget about this one," I said. "We need a picture of you."

"I don't have one," Raymond said.

"Do you have any film left in your camera?"

Raymond checked. "One more picture."

I picked up the Polaroid camera and aimed it at Raymond. He smiled. I took the picture. It slid out of the camera, dark and murky. A few minutes later, it developed in front of our eyes.

I pasted it in the book, with the secret underneath. "*Now* we have everybody."

I gave it a gold star.

The next day, we carried the secret notebook through the woods to the Secret Tree. The secrets belonged to Crazy Ike. We decided to return them to him in a Secret Ceremony.

"O Crazy Ike," I said in a low, serious voice that I thought would be appropriate for a Secret Ceremony. "O Craziest of Ikes. We present these secrets to you. Keep them well, and let them be whispered on the wind."

"Yes, O Crazy Ike," Raymond said. "I hope you're hungry."

I dropped the notebook into the hole, but it wouldn't go all the way down. Something was blocking it.

I reached inside and felt around. I touched something soft and squishy. I yanked it out.

"The voodoo doll!" Paz's face was still taped to the head, but all the pins were gone.

"That means the curse is really over," Raymond said.

I put the notebook into the hole and stuffed the doll in with it. "That ought to keep you full for a while, Crazy Ike," Raymond said.

The ship's bell rang. Mom was calling us home.

We bowed before the Secret Tree and ran home through the woods. Mr. Gorelick waited for us on his front steps.

"Get your harmonicas, kids. I feel like playing a round."

Raymond and I sat down with Mr. Gorelick and played this song:

Make new friends, but keep the old,
One is silver and the other gold.
A circle's round, it has no end,
That's how long I will be your friend.

HARMONICA

If you have a harmonica in the key of C, you can play this song. The numbers correspond to the numbers marking the holes on your harmonica. Blow into the hole as noted. When the number has a minus sign (-) in front of it, that means draw in on that hole rather than blow out. With a little practice, you'll soon be playing a tune.

Make New Friends

4   3   4   -4   5   5 5 -4
Make new friends, but keep the o-old

6 6 6 -6 6 -5 5 -4   4
One is sil-ver and the o-ther gold.

4   3   4   -4 5   5 5 -4
A circle's round, it has no e-end

6   6 6 -6 6 -5 5 -4   4
That's how lo-ong I will be your friend.